Sexy AS SIN

LAS VEGAS SERIES

wildflowers & WHISKEY

AMBITION & PASSION ALWAYS BURN BRIGHT

SARA MCCLAFLIN

First Edition

ASIN: B0DV46SD5Y

ISBN (trade): 979-8-9991778-0-3

Book Cover: Pia

Editing: Brandy Gibson

Social Media Coordinator: Tawny Gratto

Social Media Group Moderator: Ashley Sullivan

PA: Sarah Toon

Marketing & PR: Wildfire Marketing Solutions

Content Warning

This book contains mature content and situations intended for adult readers (18+). Some of the events, conflicts, or character backstories may touch on sensitive topics.

Reader discretion is strongly advised.

If you'd like to see a detailed list of possible triggers and content notes before you begin, I've prepared one for you on my website: https://www.authorsaramcclaflin.com/wildflowers-and-whiskey

CHAPTER 1

Frankie

THAT'S IT. NO MORE ALCOHOL, NEVER AGAIN. MY head feels like it's swimming in an ocean of shit.

I groan, roll over, and slap a pillow over my eyes hoping to block out the sun. News flash. It never works.

I crack one eye open. Then the other, blinking a couple of times.

This room looks...different.

Floor to ceiling windows that overlook the Strip—first clue. The second? That my entire apartment could fit in this one room. Twice.

I push myself up slowly and rub my eyes. Something cold hits my cheek.

A ring.

A diamond ring.

Big enough to have its own zipcode. On *my* ring finger.

Well shit.

I stare at it willing it to disappear.

"No," I mutter. "No way I was *that* drunk."

But it looks like I was.

Because I have no idea whose bed this is. Or who the fuck I *married*.

"Damnit, Frankie," I mutter to myself. "You promised that you would never get this drunk again."

I toss the ridiculously soft blankets off and get to my feet. I am wearing a man's shirt. Great. *Classy, Frankie, just so classy.*

Whoever it is has money. And lots of it. That's the only kind of man who lives in a place that looks like a penthouse in Las Vegas.

I make a beeline for the windows. I know this view— high, central, Strip facing. Stellan had this view before he traded his penthouse for a picture perfect picket fence home with his wife, Talia.

Okay so I know *where* I am

Still don't know *why* I'm in Beckett's room though. That's when I hear the clanging in the kitchen. It's now or never.

I scan the room for my dress. I spot it draped over the bench at the foot of the bed, my heels tipped over underneath. Last is just a giant blackhole. I remember Talia and Stellan's official wedding, champagne, dancing, a dare I definitely shouldn't have taken.

I shimmy into my dress, grab my bag, my shoes, and inch toward the door.

The last thing that I want to do is an awkward goodbye or having to look at the person I married.

I slip into the hallway and shut the door with a soft click.

For just a second, I'm disoriented. The area tilts on its side until it all comes back to focus.

Padding to the front door, heels in hand, I stop dead in my tracks.

A warm, broad hand extends in front of my line of sight. It's holding a steaming cup of coffee.

"Going somewhere, my love?" My stomach flips. I know that voice. The deep timber and the tone. Beckett. Fucking. Harrington.

I look down at his hands. Coffee just the way I like to drink it—splash of cream and a hint of cinnamon. And... and a... ring on his finger.

No.

No, no, no.

I lift my eyes hoping and praying with everything in me that I'm wrong.

But there he is—tousled hair, shirtless, stubble on his jaw. Relaxed in a way I haven't seen him in a long time. The look on his face isn't a smug one. More like shy.

I take the mug and sip without thinking. Of course it's perfect. Of course he would remember exactly how I take it. He's always noticed the little things. Even if I didn't want him to.

That's when it hits me.

Not the caffeine.

My love.

I choke. Spit coffee back into the cup like he just poisoned me. The splitting feeling in my head comes back as the broken memories rush back. Flashes of light and alcohol at Talia and Stellan's reception.

Champagne galore. Way too much of it. Cal whispering something... probably something outrageous. A dare? Maybe?

No. A goddamn chapel.

Neon lights. Staggered words? No, vows. Us laughing. A blur of silk flowers shoved in my hands and signing a piece of paper. I wrack my brain for what that could be.

My only conclusion is it's a marriage license. So this is real.

I look up at his face—Beckett's face—being the only one I can remember clearly.

Oh, fuck.

"We didn't..." I manage. "Tell me we didn't."

His smile drops. His face turns serious. "Didn't what?"

"Get married." I'm pleading now. I don't know what I want more. The truth or for him to lie to me. "Tell me we didn't."

He just looks at me. He says nothing. He studies me like he's looking for me to tell him that I'm okay with all of this.

"We did." His tone is matter-of-fact, like someone who just scheduled a meeting or confirming a memo. Not someone whose life has been upheaved and turned upside down by a drunken mistake.

I can barely look at him. But I can't stop staring at him either. He's a corporate ice kind. Buttoned up legacy heir. And my personal nemesis.

"I can't," I whisper, pressing the mug back into his hands like it's about to explode. "I can't do this."

I try to move past him, but throws a hand out, stopping me. Setting the cup of coffee on the hall table, he grips my arm and pulls me in close.

"Frankie—" His tone is placating, like he's talking to a scared animal about to bolt.

"No." My voice starts to shake. Everything is culminating to the surface and I'm about to break. "I don't remember. Any of it! Not the night. Or vows. Not why we even did this to ourselves. Just that it happened—and now we're here—and I can't breathe."

He pulls me into his chest with his left hand going to the back of my head. He's comforting me. And it's actually kind of working. I'm going to have an anxiety attack.

"Frankie, stop. Relax. Everything is going to be—"

"Don't even finish that sentence, Beckett. *Don't.*"

I yank myself back, pulling away from him. I see something like disappointment flicker in his eyes. But what was he expecting? Everything to be happy and perfect?

"I need space. I need air. I need... fuck, I need a damn time machine."

I start to pace the hallway. I need to move, walk, run, scream, *something*. I need to figure out what to do.

"You really think I'd get married on a whim? That I wouldn't be sure about it?" His voice is deceptively low. He's trying to maintain composure.

"That's exactly my problem!" I can't help it, I just snap, walking back to him. "I think a small part of me wanted to be with you too. Just not like this."

My jaw tightens and I will the tears into place. I will not cry right now.

"You're a good guy," I say, my voice cracking around the edges. "Too good for this mess and a disaster like me."

Then I run. As fast as I can, without looking back. Shoes in hand. Adrenaline on high.

What the hell did I just do?

CHAPTER 2
Beckett

I CAN DO NOTHING BUT WATCH HER LEAVE. I should've seen this coming. Her confusion and fear all wrapped up in a fucked up package tied with a pretty bow.

I can't get her out of my head. Hell, I couldn't get her out of my head when I moved to New York six years ago.

I had the worst possible reaction to her confession, I know that.. She told me she loved me. I said she was too young. That's how I felt. What I didn't say was that I loved her too. I've never stopped.

Frankie DeLuca is special. She is beautiful, smart, and funny as hell.

She's my everything. She just doesn't know it yet. But she will.

I've been watching her since returning from the east coast. She is vibrant and vivacious.

I wasn't drunk at all last night. I nursed the same beer all night long. She started staying with me because of her flooded apartment and I wanted to make sure I didn't miss a moment of our time together, no matter the circumstances.

I remember everything. Not just the vows. Not just the ring.

I remember *her*.

She doesn't just walk into the room. She arrives. Like a switch flipped, lighting up the space the moment she stepped through the door. All heads turn towards her.

The kind of beautiful that is devastating. Confidence blooms with every step that she takes. Her smile hits me right in the chest.

I can't help, but to watch every move she makes. Every step. Every turn of her head. Like she's the center of gravity and I'm already off balance.

I try to rub the ache in my heart. Her eyes are moving through the room. She's looking for some fun. The glint in her eyes gives it all away.

She walks straight up to the bar. Cal notices her first. Of course he did.

Cal notices everyone. He's smooth, funny, impossible not to like. The kind of man who flirts with anything that breathes, and somehow never gets slapped for it.

He leans in and whispers something into her ear. She tips her head back and lets out a boisterous laugh that I can imagine the sound over the beat of the music. My eyes follow her hand and as it taps his chest, flicking his collar. He laughs at something she says.

It's playful. It's familiar. It still makes something tighten in my chest.

And then she turns. Eyes scanning, unfocused—until they land on me.

She stumbles over, drink in hand, grin too big, heels forgotten somewhere along the way. She smells like champagne and citrus and heat. Like trouble that already knows it's been caught.

"Cal asked me out," she slurs, leaning into my space like she owns it. "I said yes."

I don't move. I'm frozen in place. She didn't just say what I thought she did.

"No." That one word flies out of my mouth so fast I couldn't stop it.

She laughs loudly. "You can't say that."

"I just did."

She tips her head back, sighing like I've just annoyed her so much she can't comprehend any of it.

"You don't get to say no. You—" She jabs a finger at my chest. "You could've had me, Beckett. Every bit of me." She giggles at her own words. "But you said no. Remember?"

I remember. Every second.

I put down the beer I've let get warm and grab her hand.

"Where are we going?" She stumbles along behind me. Clearly she's absolutely wasted.

"Home," I say. She can barely stand on her feet. "You're hammered."

She grins like she's proud of it. Hair falling loose around her face, makeup smudged just slightly—and somehow, she looks even better like this. She is wild and free. Not tamed by what is going on around her.

"You're not listening."

"I am," I say, grabbing her glass and setting it on the table next to me. "That's why I'm calling it."

The Strip pulses around us—hot lights, distant bass, the scent of asphalt and sugar and cigarette smoke. She sways slightly, but her eyes are locked ahead.

She stops walking and her fingers tighten on mine.

I follow her gaze.

The chapel is drenched in neon. Pink hearts, plastic roses, a glowing sign that says 'Happily Ever After Starts Here.' The front doors are propped open like they're waiting for someone dumb enough to walk through.

She tilts her head, grinning at me with all a smile that says she has a really bad idea. "Let's get married."

I stare at her. "What?"

She turns to me. "You heard me."

"Frankie—"

"No. Listen." She steps in closer. Her eyes are wide and glassy, but her voice is serious. As serious as a drunk person could be. "You're always in control. Always thinking. Don't you ever get tired of it?"

My heart is thudding too loud in my chest. I can count the beats.

"Just once," she whispers, fingers brushing my jaw. "Be reckless with me."

I should walk away. I should take her home, put her in bed, and pretend this never happened. But then she bites her bottom lip and looks up at me like I'm the only person on the busy Vegas Strip.

So I let her pull me inside.

A lady pops out from behind the counter. She gives us a chart of different ceremonies and add ons.

I don't even look at the numbers. Just hand over the card.

"Want to take a look at them?" he asks.

"No," I say, in a bit of disbelief. "Just give her whatever she wants."

The lady gives me a look—somewhere between impressed and mildly alarmed—as the receipt prints.

I slide an extra bill across the counter. A big one. Maybe too big. It doesn't matter. The only thing that does matter is the smile on her face.

Frankie's already spinning under the plastic arch, arms out, laughing like she owns the night.

I'd buy this moment a thousand times over if I could. I'd give her everything I've ever had just to keep her smiling at me like that.

We sign the papers first. Her handwriting is a disaster—a heart and a star and something that might be a crown.

She squints at it, grinning. "You sign like a man. Someone with something to hide. Maybe I can be your little secret now."

She's wrong. She's never been a secret. She's been the center of everything I've tried to deny.

The officiant gestures for us to walk down the aisle. She loops her arm through mine and leans in close.

"You nervous?" Frankie asks, tipping her head up at me, eyes glinting mischief under smeared mascara.

"Terrified," I admit it even though I don't want to.

She grins, pleased. "Hot."

She's glowing. Her lipstick's smudged. Her hair is falling out of its pins. She looks like a wish someone dared to make real. I don't think I've ever loved anything more.

The officiant beams at us like we're the sweetest thing he's seen all week.

"All right, lovebirds," he says. "Time for vows."

Frankie clears her throat, swaying a little.

"I vow," she starts, swaying a little as she points a finger at me, "to occasionally turn your life upside down... but like, in a hot way."

She grins. "I vow to drink all your good liquor and replace it with shitty tequila you'll pretend not to notice. I vow to call you out when you're being a smug bastard—especially during dinner. And I vow to never, ever let you forget that you got down on one metaphorical knee in Vegas and followed me into a chapel to spend eternity together."

She pauses and looks at me just under her brow. "And I

guess... I vow to never stop making your life a little louder. A little messier. More grand than you ever thought it could be."

I laugh—not because what she said was funny. But because there was truth in every bit of it. Her words are what makes me love her more.

"Your turn, soon to be husband," she says, all slurred and smug.

She is baiting me. Like she wants me to compete with her on our vows. Because everything is a contest to her.

"I vow to never make you feel lesser than," I say quietly. "To never ask you to dim the parts of you that shine so bright in a way no one else would ever understand."

She startles, stumbling back just a bit in a way where I have to hold her up.

"I vow to carry it—all of it—when you're tired of carrying it alone. I vow to see you when no one else does. And to never stop being stupidly, completely in love with you... even if you forget this whole night."

Her eyes go glassy. "Fuck, that was good."

The officiant announces us married. And she doesn't wait. She crashes into me, hands in my hair, mouth on mine, and I kiss her like I've wanted to for the last six years.

"Mr. and Mrs. Harrington," the officiant says in the background.

She pulls back, breathless. "Mr. and Mrs. Fuckaround-and-Find-Out," she corrects proudly. "Tell the galaxy."

She stumbles—just a little. I catch her by the waist, but the spark in her eyes is already fading. She's starting to fade.

"Okay," she murmurs. "Now I'm tired. Husband, take me home."

"Gladly."

We take a cab back to Onyx. She's already starting to fall asleep. There's no way she'll be able to walk in without help.

I pay the driver and help her out of the car. The ring I bought her five years ago glints on her finger—finally where it was always meant to be. I kept hers on me for years. It's been part of me through moves, meetings, even an international flight. It became less of a ring and more of a habit. Like breathing.

The elevator ride to the penthouse is quiet. She leans against me, heels swinging from one hand, the marriage certificate clutched in the other like a prized possession. I type the code in with my free hand.

"Penthouse at the Onyx," she mutters, stepping inside like she's afraid of making it dirty. "Must be nice being Rothwell royalty."

"You're Mrs. Royalty now. Half of this is yours."

She spins to face me, one brow raised. "Great. I'll take the closet, the bar, and the bed. You can keep the mirrors and whatever soulless art that is. Except for these. They are mine."

I turn around and look at what she's referring to. The Ophelia Duvain originals. Some of the only pieces that make me feel. They remind me of her, which is why I bought them.

"Deal," I chuckle, looking at her once again.

She yawns, dropping her heels and certificate on the entry table. I walk her to the master bedroom.

She sits on the bed and lays down. I change while she mumbles to herself.

I hand her a shirt. She doesn't ask. Just strips out of the dress, doesn't even flinch. The shirt is going to be bigger than she is.

I look away. Not because I don't want to see—God, I want to see—but because I want her to feel safe. She is too drunk to really remember anything.

"You're weirdly sweet for a man who barely cracks a smile. Ever," she mutters, tugging the shirt over her head.

Little does she know... I only ever smile at her.

"Get in bed, Frankie," I say.

She crawls across the mattress without grace, flopping onto the pillows with a dramatic groan. "Oh my God. This is the best bed I've ever been in."

I slide in next to her, expecting her to roll away, claim the edge, build distance. She doesn't do that at all, she turns toward me, finds me with her hands, and curls into my chest like it's muscle memory. Like we've done this a thousand times.

"You're warm," she mumbles. "I married a heater."

"Sleep," I whisper, resting my chin on her head. "I've got you."

And I do. I've got her. For tonight. For as long as she'll let me.

The door's already shut.

She's gone.

And I'm still standing here, staring at the space she tore through like I don't already know how this ends.

She thinks this was a mistake. That she can outrun it, laugh it off, forget it ever happened.

Let her try.

She's not the only one who knows how to play pretend.

She wanted this. I saw it in her eyes. Felt it in her hands. Heard it in every slurred vow she made with a smile on her face and my name on her tongue.

I'm not letting her rewrite that.

She can run. Fuck, I hope she does.

Because now?

I'm chasing.

Game on, Francine. A smirk curls my lips as I look out over the city lights.

CHAPTER 3
Frankie

WORK.

The one thing I can count on to stay sane in this mess of a world I built for myself.

The daily grind is something I can always count on. The routine of drinks and rowdy customers is my saving grace.

It's busy, thankfully, I have to keep my mind from wandering to Beckett.

"Hey, Frankie," Lena Marquez calls out as I walk in.

She's our assistant manager—sharp as a tack and always on top of everything. Between her, Roxy Lane on nights, and me covering swing shifts, we've got the dream team of management.

It works out great for me. I don't need to be in at seven in the morning.

Lena's still talking. My eyes widen just a bit as I remember the ring on my finger. I subtly slide it off, tucking it in my pocket before she can notice it. The last thing I need is people asking questions. I don't even know the answers to the questions they'll ask.

"Hey," I say quickly. "What's up?"

"Are you okay?" She looks at me suspiciously, narrowing her eyes. I'm not okay. But I can't tell her that. I don't want to have to explain.

"Yeah, I'm good," I say, hoping my voice sounds even. That would be a win for me if it does and I need the fucking win. "Roxy tell you how last night went?"

"She said it was decent," she continues, looking down to scan her clipboard. "There was an issue that security handled."

I perk up at that. My mind is focused on what she's saying. A security issue usually means I have to do an incident report.

I nod and grab all of the witness statements Roxy had employees and some bystanders fill out. She also has the note report that Roxy filled out about the incident. I escape to my office—my favorite hiding place.

It's the only part of the bar that really feels fully mine. I put warm tones with splashes of color everywhere. I shoved little momentos and nick knacks everywhere I could find a place. The couch has throw pillows. The bookshelves are lined with my favorites. The walls have art I actually love.

I hate the corporate feel. That's the office I got. This is the dream I've always wanted.

I shrug off my blazer and drop into the chair. The report states an average fight, two guests got into it, there were no actual injuries. Roxy called security, and eventually the cops.

She handled it like a pro, and didn't need any support. That's why I promoted her as soon as I could.

Once I send the incident report for the security manager to sign off on, I get right into the rest of the work I need to do. Scheduling, payroll, responding to supplier emails. The usual. When I finally glance up, almost half the day is gone.

Lena flagged some inventory issues earlier, and it's about

time I stretched my legs. I need to head out to the floor to double check the bar stock and make sure everyone is good.

But the bar is packed, way busier than it usually is at this time.

My bartenders are slammed. Barbacks are rushing around. Orders are flying off the ticket machine. I don't even think—I slide behind the bar and jump in.

This? I can do this. I'm back to what I know best.

Until I see him.

Beckett is standing in the corner of the room, holding a takeout bag from my favorite restaurant like it's no big deal. News flash… it's a fucking *huge* deal.

Of course he looks good for being hungover. Unfairly good since I feel like shit.

He's leaning against the wall in a dark blue suit minus the tie. His jacket is draped over his arm. How is his hair so perfect yet messy at the same time?

Snap out of it, Frankie!

Interesting. It doesn't look like he went to work today. More like he wanted to be here instead of anywhere else.

That he came here just for me. And I really don't like that.

I walk toward him, stomach fluttering, already mad at myself for feeling anything at all.

"What are you doing here?"

"You need to eat, love," he says, like it's the most obvious thing in the world.

My heart skips a beat. Stupid fucking thing can stop.

"I'm fine," I say.

"I know you are," he sighs. "I just want to take care of you. Is that a crime now?"

I don't answer. Just turn and lead him to my office. Suddenly my small sanctuary feels suffocating and too small with the both of us in it.

"Where is your ring?" He frowns, his expression stormy for a moment before he catches himself and looks at me with confusion.

I pull it from my pocket and hold it out, like evidence. Like proof that I haven't forgotten. Until I see it—*his* ring. On his finger.

"Yours is still on," I say.

"I was never planning on taking it off," he says in a way that turns my world on its head.

We eat in silence. Awkward silence. This is new. We've never had awkwardness between us. Only mutual annoyance. Or what I thought was mutual. Now I'm not sure.

But everything is different now.

We're married. Legally bound to one another.

My head says annulment, just break it off cleanly. We could go back to how we were before all of this shitstorm.

But my fucking heart is still standing in the chapel, drunk, and jumping for joy at our I dos.

This is not the time or place for the conversation we need to have. Not here. Not now. We need to talk... and that time is coming very soon.

I don't know if I'm ready. Not when I've waited for this for so long.

I trusted him once and he crushed me heart and soul. I can't let it happen again.

I just turned twenty one today. Stellan is throwing me a huge party. Of course, his friends are here too.

I look around for Beckett. He is the one and only person I want to be here. The one that I've always wanted to be with.

I think I fell in love with him the first second I saw him. Eighteen, just left home, and moved in with Stellan. Beckett came over for dinner and talked to me like a human, not some kid.

I sit on a bench in the back of the room. I may like a good party, but this is a lot for me.

I feel movement on the other end of the plush bench. Turning, I see Beckett sitting there. He's smiling at me. I want to say it's only for me, that he feels a fraction of what I do for him.

"Hey," he says, sliding closer. "Why are you sitting over here by yourself? You do know this party is for you, right?"

"I needed to be off of my feet and away from everyone for a bit," I say, smiling back.

We sit next to each other for a few minutes, but it feels like an eternity while I wrestle with my thoughts.

The words build in my chest. Maybe they're brave. But it's probably stupid, in reality.

"I'm glad you came," I say, turning to face him. "I was hoping you would."

"I wouldn't miss it," he says, and the way he looks at me? God, it makes my heart trip.

Something in me cracks. It's my birthday. I know exactly what I want. If I don't say it now, I never will.

"I'm in love with you."

His smile drops.

And for half a second, I think he might say it back. I'm willing him to say it back. It's right there.

But then I see the indecision on his face. The scrunch of his brow and sigh coming out of his mouth. This is not going to end well for me.

"Frankie..."

It's the way he says it. Like I'm a little kid... a girl and not the woman I am.

"You're twenty one," he says, eyes full of pity dressed as concern. "You're still figuring things out."

A hot knife of anger slices through me aiming right at my

heart. I gasp. I can barely breathe. The last thing I want is someone telling me that I'm not ready.

"You think I don't know what I want?"

"You think I'm what you want," he says. "That's not the same."

I shoot to my feet, he will not make me out to be a child. I know who I am. I know who I want. Although, that has changed. Because I don't want someone who is disrespecting me like he is right now.

His gaze follows me, but he doesn't stop my movements away from him. He doesn't reach, doesn't fight, he does nothing as I walk away. That solidifies my decision that I am better than him.

"Frankie, wait," he says.

I laugh. Now he wants me to wait? To what? Talk it out? Give him more time to convince me I'm wrong?

"Go to hell, Beckett."

I walk away. Head high. Back straight. Even if my heart feels like it just shattered across the goddamn floor.

I deserve better. Better than Beckett Harrington.

I push back from my desk and stand abruptly.

"I need to go, it's busy out there," I say, voice tight. "Thank you for lunch."

"Wait." He reaches out, trying to stop me. Like that would even be possible. "I thought we could talk. For just a minute."

"About what, Beckett?" My anger rises. Frustration in my chest bubbles to the surface. The cracks at the edge of my vision appear. "What do you *want* from me?"

"Us," he says. "Our relationship. What happens next—"

"There *is* no relationship," I cut him off. "We are getting an annulment or divorce. Or whatever legal reset button we need to hit to erase this mess."

"Frankie—" I can see his heartbreak. He looks like a puppy, it's almost enough to make me sit back down. *Almost.*

"No!" I shake my head, rubbing my temples. "You don't get to say my name. Not like that. You lost that right a long time ago."

He moves before I can stop him—arms wrapping around me, pulling me close. I can hear his heartbeat in my ear.

I hate how much I love this. How good it feels. It's so reminiscent of when he used to hug me. I want to melt into him and forget everything. Trust him again.

Putting me at arms length, he leans down to gently kiss my cheek.

"I'll see you later," he says, softly. His lips tracing the shell of my ear.

This time it's him that leaves me standing alone. Breathless and shaken to the core.

What the *fuck* am I supposed to do now?

CHAPTER 4
Beckett

FOR THE FIRST TIME IN MY LIFE, I'M LOST. NOT metaphorically.

I'm fully, viscerally lost. Because I don't know how to keep her. I need to. I feel it deep in my bones that I need her.

Frankie.

She's in my lungs now, in my bloodstream. She's the background noise to every second of my day.

I know I fucked this up six years ago. I could have stayed. I could have fought. But that is the past and not the present.

That look she gave me before I left completely gutted me. Hell, she barely even looked at me. Like I am diseased and she can't stand to be around me.

I've closed billion dollar deals while enemies circled like sharks. I've made decisions that could level companies. I don't waver. Ever

This moment is different. This decision is different. Those deals never have my heart on the line. Not like this. She holds my bleeding, beating heart in her soft, perfect hands.

I go into work because it's what I know. It's muscle memory. But it doesn't matter.

I stare at numbers I usually read like a natural language and can't retain a single one. I nod through meetings I called and couldn't tell you what anyone said.

Because all I can see is her. The life we could have.

Frankie, barefoot in my kitchen, lips curled around the rim of her coffee mug. Frankie, in my bed, tangled in a shirt I gave her. Frankie, looking at me like maybe—just maybe—I was who she chooses to be with.

I'm just supposed to sit at my desk like any of this feels normal? Unfortunately it looks to be that way.

ONYX is humming today. Everyone's moving. I'm the only one that is offcenter.

My office isn't glass and metal and ego. It's dark wood, low light, leather armchairs no one ever uses but me. A record player sits under the window with a stack of vinyl in the corner. I like the space to feel lived in.

I've got reports open in front of me. Projections, contracts, strategy maps. All things I usually devour. Today they're meaningless. Today I can't stop picturing the shape of her in my bed.

I think about her not wearing her ring. She had it in her pocket, like some kind of shame that she has to hide. It makes me wonder if I am a shameful person she wants to hide away like dirty laundry.

It's not that I'm afraid of feeling this. I've never been afraid of emotion. Emotion tells you what matters.

She matters more than I've ever let her see. But that's about to change. She's about to know everything.

I glance out the window, down at the Strip. People are moving fast from place to place. Bright lights and louder lives. I'm ready to slow down. Follow Stellan's footsteps. Find my person and never let her go.

There's a knock at the door, jolting me from my thoughts.

"Come in," I say without looking up.

The door swings open, and Cal saunters in like he has nowhere better to be. His usual swagger speaks to the fact that he believes he belongs in any room he steps into. He shuts the door behind him and drops into the chair across from my desk without waiting to be invited.

"I figured I'd find you in here," he says, propping his ankle on his knee. "You look like hell, by the way."

I grunt. "Thanks."

He leans forward, scanning me. "Alright, what gives? You've had the lovesick look before, but this is some next level brooding."

I don't say anything. He follows my gaze to where my hand rests on the desk—and freezes.

"...Wait."

I glance at him.

His eyes are locked on my left hand. "Beckett. What the hell is *that*?"

I lift my hand slightly, like this is a completely obvious visual. "A ring."

"No shit, Sherlock." His voice pitches up. "Is that what I think it is?"

I nod once. "It's exactly what you think it is."

Cal blinks. "You—*you* got married? Who—wait. No." He shakes his head. "Tell me you didn't—"

"Frankie."

He exhales hard. "Jesus Christ."

I don't respond.

"You married Frankie?" he asks, voice lower now, like he's trying to make sense of the words out loud. "Like, legally? Full vows, signature and everything?"

"Full ceremony. Witnessed. Chapel on the Strip."

Cal leans back, runs a hand through his hair. "Holy *shit.* You—*when?*"

"After Talia and Stellan's. That night."

Cal stares at me. "You were hammered."

"I wasn't."

His eyes widen. "You're saying you—*you knew what you were doing?*"

"Yes."

Silence stretches between us.

He shakes his head slowly. "You married the girl you've been pining over for six years—on a whim—and *you weren't even drunk?*"

I let that sit in the air. "I've never been more sure of anything in my life."

Cal whistles low. "Damn. And she?"

"She was drunk. But she woke up in my bed and had questions. She knows now." I know that my voice is cracking. I can't help it. When I say it outloud, it sounds absolutely crazy. I sound insane.

What's worse? The fact that I am admitting it to Cal. Or that it happened.

His voice softens. "How'd she take it?"

"She left."

Cal winces. "Ah."

"And said we're getting it annulled."

"Are you?" Cal asks quietly. He knows I'm being vulnerable about this whole thing.

"I'm not letting her go," I say.

"You've loved her for years," he says, like it's the simplest truth in the world.

"Every version of her," I admit, the words thick in my throat.

"And if she runs?" he asks.

I meet his gaze without blinking. "I chase."

Cal grins like the Cheshire Cat. "Took you long enough." He pushes up from the chair with a mock salute. "Go get your girl, Harrington."

I nod, but my heart's already thudding. He closes the door behind him, and the silence that follows is deafening.

I glance at the clock. She'll be off work soon.

I grab my jacket, shove my laptop in my bag, and head for the elevator.

Every second closer to seeing her feels like a countdown. Let her yell. Let her glare. Just let her stay.

Because this time, I'm going to tell her I want to have a real relationship. And she's not leaving until we come to an agreement.

She's already home when I get back to the penthouse. Standing by the windows, arms wrapped tight around herself like the city might swallow her whole if she moves.

I drop my keys gently. "Hey."

She turns slowly, her eyes tired but open. But I can tell that she is tense. Worried about tonight.

"I just want to talk," I say, careful not to get too close too fast, like I'm approaching an injured animal. "No pressure. No expectations."

She nods. So I take a step closer. "I've been thinking about it a lot. About us. About everything I want in my life."

Her lips press into a thin line. "Yeah."

I motion toward the kitchen. "Can I make you tea? Or pour a drink?"

"Tea," she says quietly.

We settle into the living room, mugs warm in our hands. It's the first time since the wedding that she's not running— or I'm not chasing.

"You know I didn't plan this," I start. "The chapel. The rings. But I meant every second of it."

Her eyes lift. That surprises her.

"I was sober, Frankie. I remember everything." I pause. "You pulled me out into the Strip, laughing like the world was yours. I followed. I'll always follow"

She sips her tea. Still quiet.

"I don't want to undo it," I say. "This marriage. I want to *know* you, the way I should've tried years ago. The way I should've never stopped wanting to."

She finally meets my gaze.

"I'm not asking for our relationship to be solidified today," I say, trying to keep my composure. "I'm asking for a shot. To try. To start something real."

She watches me for a long beat. Her hands tighten around the mug. Then she sets it down, quiet and slow, like she's bracing for the blow.

"Why?" Her voice is paper thin. I can hear the shake to it.

Something in me splits wide open. I can't stop the words from spilling out.

"Because it's always been you." My chest tightens. "Because I see you in every version of my future. Because no one has ever come close to making me feel like you do."

Her lips part, but no words come out.

"You think this is about a drunken wedding?" I say, stepping closer. "Frankie, I would've married you if you asked. I would've dropped to one knee in front of the whole Strip if I thought for one second you'd say yes."

Her breath catches.

"When you told me you loved me—years ago—I wanted to say it back. God, I did. But I was scared. Not of you. Of what it would mean to love you and lose you. You were bright

34

and young and unshakable, and I was already half in love with you and convinced I'd ruin it."

She shakes her head, eyes glassy.

"But I never stopped loving you," I say, my voice breaking now. "Not for a single second. Not when you avoided me. Not when you laughed at someone else's joke. Not even when I watched you walk away."

"Beckett," she breathes. And it sounds like a prayer.

"I love every version of you. The reckless, the brave, the angry, the soft. The girl who kissed me in Vegas and the woman who's standing in front of me right now, trying not to fall apart."

Tears slip down her cheek, and I catch them with my thumbs. My hands are on her face now, my breath is shaky.

"I still love you," she whispers, barely audible.

I don't wait. I don't ask. I kiss her like she's already mine. Like the world's been on mute until this exact moment and now it's finally, finally playing the right song.

She makes a surprised sound—then melts into me. Like her heart remembered before her head did. Like her lips knew the way back to mine without a map.

We break apart, breathless and grinning. Her fingers are in my hair. My hands are on her waist like I never want to let go.

"This doesn't fix everything," she says, a slight crack in her voice.

"No," I whisper, forehead resting against hers. "But it's a hell of a place to start."

She studies me. "I want to try too."

And this time—this kiss—there's no hesitation.

It's giddy. It's golden. It's the kind of kiss that makes you believe in every stupid, beautiful love song. We're laughing into each other's mouths, dizzy with it.

Just her and me. Together at last.
Finally.

CHAPTER 5

Frankie

HE STOPS TALKING. THEN TILTS HIS HEAD, LOOKING AT me like I need to say something.

Everything I've always wanted is happening. It's all real. He wants to be with me in the way I've always dreamed. I can barely process everything that is going on. And just like that —I do fall apart. Not in pieces, but into him. I'm tired of pretending I don't feel everything when I look at him.

I don't remember who moved first. Maybe we moved at the same time. Maybe the universe finally stopped fighting us. All I know is that his mouth is on mine, and I've never felt anything like it.

My fingers tangle in his hair, tugging. His hands are every-where—my jaw, my waist, the small of my back. I fist his shirt like it's the only thing anchoring me, and then I push it up, over hard muscle and warm skin. He helps, dragging it off and tossing it to the floor.

His mouth finds my throat, and I gasp—head tilting, breath catching. He bites just enough to make me tremble.

I reach for the buttons on my blouse, but he beats me to it. He undoes them slowly. Annoyingly slow. I want more. By the time the fabric slides off my shoulders, I'm shaking from the inside out.

"You have no idea," he growls into my neck, "how long I've wanted this."

We stumble backward. His hands find the zipper at the side of my skirt and tug it down without looking. It puddles around my feet a second later.

I step out of it and pull his belt free in one practiced motion. He groans—deep—and my entire body clenches.

The back of my knees hit the wall first. Then the console table. Then, *finally,* my back hits the bedroom door.

He presses me there, pinning me with nothing but his body and a look that says he's just as gone as I am.

He slides his hands under the barely there lace of my underwear, holding me like I'm his to remember.

"Tell me to stop," he murmurs into my neck, breath hot. But his hands are trembling. Like he already knows I won't.

I look him dead in the eye and whisper, "Don't you dare."

And that's it.

He lifts me effortlessly and I wrap my legs around his waist, our mouths colliding again as the door clicks shut behind us.

Inside, it's a blur of skin and hands and half shed clothes. My bra hits the floor first, then his pants. My underwear next. His breath hitches when he sees me fully, like he's been waiting his whole life just to look.

Clothes come off like they're the only thing standing in our way. Like if we strip everything away—every layer, every wall—then maybe we'll finally have a shot at something real.

His mouth drags down my neck, slow and claiming, like he's laying a map of every inch of me. My hands fist in his shirt before I shove it off completely.

I've thought about this—fantasized, dreamed, *ached* for

this. And now that he's here, real and looking at me like I'm the only thing he's ever wanted, I'm done pretending I don't want it just as bad.

"Still with me?" he murmurs, lips brushing just under my jaw.

I bite back a moan. "I'm the one pressed against the door, Beckett. I think I'm *very* with you."

He growls roughly and it shoots straight through me. "That mouth is going to get you in trouble."

I hook a leg around his hip. "Maybe I should use it more."

His eyes flash dark, like I flipped a switch. "You have *no* idea what you just asked for."

Oh, but I do. His gaze drags down me like worship, like he's seeing something holy.

"You're going to be the death of me," he says.

I lean in, lips brushing his. "That's the plan."

His fingers slide between my thighs, slow and smooth and *perfect*, and I can't help the noise that escapes me.

"There she is," he says against my mouth, smiling hard. "My favorite sound."

I tug at his waistband. "Less talking. More doing."

He laughs and lifts me like I weigh nothing. My back hits the mattress before I can even breathe.

Beckett's body covers mine before I've even landed. His chest is hot against my breasts, his hard cock pressing between my thighs—and I ache for him. My legs fall open instinctively, welcoming him, the stretch of him, the promise of everything we've both been starving for.

His hands skim up my ribs, tracing every curve like he's burning it into memory. He cups my face, reverent, and then kisses me again—tongue sliding deep, taking, giving, hungry.

Teeth graze my lower lip, and I gasp, threading my fingers into his hair and tugging until he groans into my mouth.

"You feel like a dream," he breathes against me. "I keep thinking I'll wake up and this'll be gone."

My nails score down his back, his muscles shifting beneath my hands. He trails kisses down my throat, over the peaks of my breasts, down my stomach.

His mouth returns to mine in a kiss that steals the air from my lungs, and his cock—thick, hot, already leaking—presses against my slick folds. I whimper, lifting my hips, desperate for him.

"Now," I pant. "Beckett, now."

He lines up and pushes in so slow that I almost scream at him to move faster. I gasp as he stretches me open, inch by thick inch, until he's fully buried inside me, cock pulsing, every nerve sparking.

"Fuck," he groans. "You feel like everything."

We move together—his thrusts slow, grinding, deep. His pelvis presses into my clit with each stroke. Heat builds, pressing, urgent.

His pace starts to piss me off and I make a decision. Time to show him what I want.

I catch his gaze, slide my hands under his shoulders, and push him flat onto his back. Beckett makes a surprised noise, but doesn't resist. His eyes darken.

I settle on top, sliding my pussy over him, the wet friction sending a shiver through my spine. I run my hands up and down his chest. From here, I control the rhythm.

I ride him hard and fast, rolling my hips with purpose, slamming down onto his cock as he fills me over and over. The rhythm is wild, desperate—each movement claiming him, owning him, until all I can feel is the heat, the stretch, the way he groans my name like a prayer.

"Yeah," he murmurs, "just like that."

He grasps my hips, urging me faster, deeper. His hands

roam my back, my waist, my thighs. I lean forward, lips brushing his jaw, whispering his name.

The angle shifts as I lean forward, pressing down, forcing him deeper, every thrust creating the perfect friction and fire. Sweat glistens along our bodies, quiet moans echo in the room.

His breathing is ragged, his fingers clutching the sheets, clutching me. I feel him twitch inside me—each throb a promise.

Beckett groans, gripping my hips tight before flipping us in one fluid motion. I land beneath him with a gasp, legs falling open as he drives back into me—deep, fast, desperate. His need is raw now, every thrust wild and focused, chasing his own undoing.

"Fuck, Frankie," he growls, bracing his arms beside my head. "You're gonna ruin me."

His mouth crashes into mine, all tongue and teeth and heat, his hips slamming into mine, cock hitting deep as he chases that final edge. I rake my nails down his back, crying out again as the aftershocks ripple through me.

He jerks once, twice, then stills with a broken moan, spilling inside me, his body trembling against mine. His forehead drops to mine, breath hot and ragged, and for a moment, we don't move.

I don't think I could move anywhere even if I tried.

I smile, breath still uneven. "It's never felt like this before."

Beckett strokes my lower back, his voice low and full of something I can't name. "Want to feel it again?"

I look over my shoulder, catch that glint in his eyes. Mischief lines the corner of his eyes, but love shows through.

I nod, grinning.

He shifts behind me, kisses the curve of my spine, and positions me again.

A gasp escapes me as his hands grip my hips, steady and sure.

And as we move together again, the world narrows to the rhythm of us—heat, breath, skin, want—until everything else disappears.

CHAPTER 6
Frankie

I'M COMFORTABLE IN BECKETT'S ARMS.

Typically, I hate cuddling. But there seems to be a lot that I enjoy when it's with him.

I shift, trying to will myself to fall back asleep. It's my day off, and I plan to take full advantage of it.

Until my phone buzzes. I groan, reaching for it blindly.

Six missed calls. Lena. Roxy too.

Fuck.

ROXY

> Hey, Franks. I know that it's your day off, but we have something going on at the bar.
> Need you ASAP.

This was sent an hour ago. *Double fuck.*

LENA

> Roxy stayed. It's not making a difference.
> We need you.

Panic sparks. I sit up, my heart hammering in my chest.

I throw on whatever I can find, brushing my teeth and quickly dragging a brush through my hair. I need to leave a note—or something for Beckett—but I'm already out the door. I'll just text him when I get there.

They have never called me on a day off. I trained them to be able to handle anything. If they're reaching out like this, it's bad.

The elevator from the penthouse is painfully slow. I pace the walls like a tiger trapped in a cage.

What if someone got hurt? A robbery? A fire?

The second the doors open, I bolt. Running until I get to the bar without stopping.

The bar looks like a warzone.

Shattered glass litters the floor. Tables are overturned. Security trying—and failing—to restore order.

That's when I hear the shriek.

"Where is that bitch?!" The woman's screeching like she's possessed by something.

I push further into the room. Lena and Roxy are off to the side, tense and pale.

"Hey," I say, coming up behind them. "What the hell is going on?"

They both look at me. Their eyes are wide. The look of fear running through each of their expressions has a flash of fear of my own rushing through me.

"These two got here at like three or four and are still screaming," Lena says, scanning the room nervously. "Something about Beckett and demanding to speak to the woman living in his penthouse."

A snap of panic washes over me before I take a deep breath and get my shit together. I haven't told anyone at work about us. I like to keep my private life private. And in Vegas, little gets around without others knowing about it.

I square my shoulders, exhale, and step toward the women who have security surrounding them. "Can I help you?" I keep my voice calm—but inside, my pulse is racing.

The taller woman looks at me, her icy gaze locked on mine while she sips a drink. Like she's appraising art and not helping the other one destroy a bar.

"We're looking for someone," she says coldly.

"Who?"

The younger one steps forward, heels clicking across the polished floor. "Francine DeLuca. Heard of her?"

Oh, so it's that kind of morning. Apparently I've been summoned.

"I want her here. Right now!" The bar flinches at her high pitched tone. "Wait... you're her. Aren't you?" The girl storms forward. Her heels click like gunshots. "You've been staying in Beckett Harrington's penthouse. We've heard the rumors."

My mouth opens, but I can't find the words fast enough.

"I just want to talk," she says with a smile that doesn't reach her eyes.

Then the crack of her hand connecting to my cheek echoes through the bar. My head whips to the side, the force jolting through my entire body. Heat blooms instantly across my face. The shock is louder than the pain at first, a white hot flush spreading under my skin.

I blink, stunned, reeling. My hand flies to my face as I stumble a step back, nearly knocking into a barstool behind me.

"Hey!" Lena shouts from behind me. "You do not lay a hand on her!"

Roxy gasps. "What the actual fuck is wrong with you?!"

"Wrong with me?" The girl scoffs. "She's the one sneaking around like some groupie."

I'm done playing nice. "Who even *are* you?"

"I'm Lorraine Collette," she says. "And this—" her hand gestures toward the furious brunette at her side "—is my daughter."

My brain stutters.

Collette.

Not just any Collette. *Lorraine* Collette. The kind of name that gets you into galas without an invitation and out of scandals without a scratch.

But everyone in this town knows the truth behind the pearls and polish.

She didn't build her empire. She married it. Chewed through three husbands with deeper wallets than backbones. Took their names, their fortunes—then walked away when their usefulness ran dry.

Now she's grooming her daughter to do the same.

The younger one—Lexi—practically radiates it, standing here with that same entitled glint in her eye, like I'm dirt under her $2,000 heels.

This isn't a mother daughter duo, it's a legacy of calculated seduction and power plays. And apparently, I've stepped right into their crosshairs.

"I'm Beckett's fiancée," Lexi spits, chin lifted like she's just slammed a gavel in court.

That is the last thing I was expecting her to say. *Fiancée?*

My stomach twists. Blood drains from my face. *No.* "What?" It comes out strangled. That's so pathetic.

She steps forward, folding her arms like she's just landed the killing blow. Her voice drips with scorn. "Don't play dumb. Everyone knows we're supposed to get married.

Everyone. And yet somehow, you're the one in his penthouse. Sleeping in his bed."

I blink, trying to process. But everything in me is screaming *no.*

Because Beckett—he never said a word. Not once. Not even a breath of this.

"I didn't know," I whisper, throat closing around the words. "He never told me—"

"Of course he didn't," Lexi sneers. "Why ruin the fantasy when he can play house with the girl no one knows? Dragged off the Strip like a cheap fucking souvenir."

Her words slap harder than her hand ever could.

She steps closer, her tone mocking now. "But hey—congrats. I broke the illusion. Whatever spell you had over him? It's done. Hope the view from the penthouse was worth it. Because your delusion is officially over."

Lexi's lips curl up at the corners. She thinks she won. But I'm just getting started. And I'm done playing nice.

"You know what's funny?" I say, tilting my head. "You're standing in *my* bar, screaming about a man who never even mentioned your name. Not once."

Lorraine stiffens.

I smile sweetly. "And you want to call *me* the homewrecker?"

I lift my hand towards them, smiling slowly as they realize what I'm displaying on the left hand. The diamond on my finger glints under the bar lights like it's laughing for me.

Lexi's eyes lock on it—and widen.

"Yeah," I say, voice hardening more than I've let it before. "We didn't just hook up. We got married."

"Liar," she snaps, but there's a crack behind it. Like she knows something is coming.

"If I'm lying, I must be *real* committed to the bit." I hold

51

the ring up again, twisting my wrist so it catches every glint of light. "Tell me something, Lexi. Did he give you a ring like this? Or just a vague promise and a seat at the kids' table?"

Lorraine's face goes pale.

"And as for being Beckett Harrington's fiancée?" I step forward, cool and deadly. "If he didn't tell me about you, maybe it's because you were never real to him. Maybe the only one who thought you were engaged was *you*."

I turn to Lorraine. "Delusion. Runs in the family, huh?"

Lexi lunges like she wants to slap me again, but I don't flinch.

"Try it," I warn. "Just know I hit back harder." Leaning back, I add, "Get out. This is my bar, my name on the license, and my husband's name on *me*. You don't belong here."

They turn to leave, and I glance at Lena—her eyes locked on the ring on my hand, wide with shock. Roxy stands beside her, smirking like she just watched her favorite TV show hit the good part.

"Oh, Francine," Lexi calls sweetly, like she's not full of shit.

I turn, just in time for the glass to fly.

It shatters against my cheek before I even register she threw it.

Sharp pain blooms across my cheekbone as the shards dig into my skin, and I stumble back, hand flying to my face. Warm, red liquid trickles down the side of my face.

Lena gasps. Roxy curses and lunges forward.

Lexi just smirks at all of us.

"That's for pretending you ever mattered," she says, her tone sweet. As sweet as arsenic. "Welcome to the big leagues, sweetheart."

The sound of footsteps at the front of the bar catches everyone's attention.

Beckett.

He steps through the entrance like a predator looking at all of his prey. He's here. He came for me. I wipe some more blood off of my face and start to make my way to him.

His expression darkens. "What the hell is going on?"

Lexi turns, feigning distress with speed so perfect. I just know she does this all of the time. "Beckett—finally! She just —came at me. She attacked us. Look what she did to my mother. I had to defend us. She did all of this to your bar!"

Lorraine clutches her pearls like this is some high society soap opera and not real life. She begins to cry on command. Wail. Like a close relative was killed in war.

I can't even process what's happening. She's lying—obviously. Beckett has to see through it. I take a step toward him, but he moves first. Not toward me. Toward her. Straight to Lexi.

He doesn't look at me. Doesn't ask if I'm okay. Doesn't even pause.

I stop in my tracks.

Lexi reaches for him, and he doesn't pull away. She leans in, whispers something I can't hear. His jaw flexes—but he doesn't correct her. Doesn't say a word.

He grabs her hand.

My stomach drops. He can't—he wouldn't.

But he's already turning, guiding her toward the door like it's a goddamn ballroom exit, not the fallout of a nightmare.

Lorraine follows, smug as ever.

Lexi looks back—right at me.

She smiles.

She won.

He chose her. What she said was true. I was nothing more than a phase he was playing house with. She was supposed to be his.

Beckett doesn't acknowledge my existence nor the blood running down my face. He doesn't even glance over his shoulder.

Not once.

Unlike him, I know how to keep a promise.

CHAPTER 7

Frankie

KEEP YOUR COMPOSURE, FRANKIE. DON'T BLOW UP.

I have to repeat that over and over in my head like a broken record. My *husband* just walked out of the bar while glass is stuck in my face and blood rushes down my cheeks without even checking if I was okay. Talk about a punch to the gut.

"Frankie!" Lena's voice cuts through the static as she pushes a wet cloth to my head.

I flinch. It burns. "That bad?"

Roxy comes over, a fresh towel in her hand. "Yeah… this isn't a butterfly bandage and a shot of tequila fix. You need stitches."

I start to feel light headed. I try to stand, but the room tilts on it's axis. Nope. Sitting is good.

"We need to get you to the hospital," Lena says.

"But the bar," I say through slurred speech.

"It needs to be cleaned anyway so let Lena and I take you to the hospital. You're the priority right now," Roxy adds.

The room sways when I blink.

Everything blurs at the edges. I can see Lena's usually

perfect bun unraveling, dark eyes full of stress, her blazer wrinkled like she's been through war. Roxy's crouched low beside her, wild streaked hair falling in her face, hazel-green eyes sharp with concern.

"I think she's gonna pass out," Roxy mutters.

And then I'm in an ambulance, Lena and Roxy beside me, not who I want... but who I need.

Turns out weekday mornings in the ER are quiet. I'm stitched up and bandaged in no time. Which would be great—if it weren't for *him*.

"Frankie?" I turn to the voice. "What are you doing here?"

I stiffen. Of course. Of *course* it's Carl Hallingsworth.

The guy my parents spent years trying to marry me off to. Blue eyes, clean white coat, arrogant posture. He's a doctor and absolutely perfect on paper, but completely and entirely wrong in every other way, every way that truly matters.

"I could ask you the same," I mutter.

He takes in the gash on my face. "What happened?"

"Comes with the territory," I respond.

He gets the hint. Mostly.

Lena appears, holding my discharge papers and all my stuff. Efficient as ever. Roxy's beside her, arms crossed, eyes already sizing Carl up.

"So," Roxy says. "When exactly were you planning on telling us you're *married*?"

I cringe. Because Carl *hears* that.

"You're married?"

I shoot him a look. "None of your business."

"Do your parents know?"

"Also not their business."

"You need to call them."

"I need to leave." I turn to Roxy. "Let's go."

"Come on, Francine," Carl sighs. "Let me look at the cut."

"Nope," Roxy steps in fast. "Back off, Doc."

"I was her fiancé," he hisses.

"You were not," I snap.

"Almost." He grabs my arm, and that's the final straw.

"Let go," I say.

"She said *let go*," Lena adds. "Unless you want me to call her husband. He'd have your job before you finish your next sentence."

"Yeah, right," Carl scoffs and rolls his eyes, focusing on the cuts on my face. "Do it."

"Lena," I say.

Lena pulls out her phone without hesitation. "Yes, hi. There's a doctor here harassing Frankie. He grabbed her arm and won't let her leave." She looks directly at Carl while she talks. "His name? Dr. Carl Hallingsworth. He seems to think Frankie doesn't have anyone looking out for her. I thought you'd want to know."

She pauses, listening, then smirks at Carl.

"Understood. Thank you, Mr. Harrington."

She hangs up and crosses her arms. "That was Frankie's husband. He's handling it. I'd suggest you leave before things get uncomfortable for you."

Carl scoffs. "You really think—"

"I think you should've walked away when you had the chance."

A new voice cuts in. "Dr. Hallingsworth," the man walks in the room in a blue suit, nothing but pure business on his face. Carl's spine straightens. "I was told you're harassing patients," the man—Dr. Kooper, his name tag reads—says.

"I'm not—"

"Hallingsworth," Roxy chuckles under her breath. "Pompous last name matches the man."

"Do you want to leave, miss?" he asks, eyes on me.

"Yes. And he won't let us."

"You're fired," Dr. Kooper says simply.

Carl gapes. "You can't—"

"I can. And I just did. Leave."

Carl looks like he might protest—then grabs my arm again. "Frankie, don't let them—"

I yank my arm away. "You did this to yourself."

He storms off, already dialing his phone. Probably my parents.

"Shouldn't have fucked with *Mrs.* Harrington," Roxy mutters.

"You're married to *Beckett Harrington*?!" Carl screams from down the hall. "No wonder you—slut like you jumps from my bed to his!"

Heads turn. The entire ER seems to pause.

Roxy smirks. "Secrets out."

Lena touches my elbow, a silent *don't*, but I shake her off.

I walk back a few steps, just enough to make sure Carl—and every witness in earshot—hears me loud and clear.

"You're right about one thing," I say. "I did *upgrade*. Drastically."

Carl opens his mouth.

"And as for the *slut* part?" I smile, playing the sweet princess he thought he was getting. "Better to be a slut than a spineless mama's boy who needed my parents to arrange his love life."

Gasps. One nurse covers her mouth. Carl's face turns a dangerous shade of red.

I tilt my head. "Have fun explaining your unemployment to your mommy."

We pile into the black SUV Lena ordered. I know they're chomping at the bit to ask me all the questions floating through their minds.

They don't wait long.

"Tell us everything," Lena says.

The car jolts over a pothole, and I wince as the bandage shifts. I can feel Roxy's eyes boring into me from the middle row.

"So, when exactly did this happen?" she asks.

I hesitate, then exhale. "After Stellan and Talia's wedding. That night."

Roxy blinks. "*That* night?"

Lena turns fully now, eyebrows raised. "So what—you left the reception and just, what, found a chapel with neon lights and said *I do*?"

"Pretty much," I mutter.

"You were drunk," Lena says carefully. "Did he... did Beckett take advantage of that? Of you?"

"No." I say it fast. Too fast maybe, but I want her to know for a fact that that isn't the case. "No, he didn't. He didn't push me into anything. It was my idea."

They both blink at me.

"I dragged him out of the hotel. I pulled him onto the Strip," I continue. "I found the chapel. I walked in. He followed me."

"You're telling me *you* proposed?" Roxy asks, somewhere between scandalized and impressed.

"I might've said, 'Let's do something crazy.'" I grimace. "And then I kissed him."

Lena raises a brow. "And he just went with it?"

"He said yes." I pause. "And the next morning, he remembered everything. But since then, we've spoken about it. We decided to stay married."

Roxy blinks. "And be together?"

"Yeah," I whisper. "He said he wanted something real. I did too. We weren't pretending."

"Shit." Lena whistles.

And Roxy exhales like she's been holding her breath for ten blocks. "Okay, well, still gonna beat his ass for today. But... damn."

"You don't have to," I say. "I'm over it."

"What do you mean?"

"He left with her," I say. "So, I can't do it anymore. I'm done." I huff out a humorless laugh and lean my head against the seat.

By the time we get back to Onyx, the sun is high, but the rain's stopped.

I thank Lena and Roxy and climb out of the Escalade. "I just need a minute," I say quickly, avoiding their eyes.

Lena doesn't push. Roxy watches me like she wants to argue, but instead just mutters, "Text us, yeah?"

I nod and head for my apartment. Thank God my key still works. The door clicks behind me, and the moment it does, my legs give out.

It's finally dry. I drop to the floor.

The tears hit hard. Like they've been waiting all morning to pour out. I press my palms into my eyes, but it's no use. I'm wrecked. Shattered in a way I didn't think was possible.

I let him in. I believed him. In him. In us.

I crawl over to the couch and grab my phone, hands shaking as I pull up Talia's contact.

She answers on the second ring, laughter in her voice.

"Hey, Franks! Give me two seconds, we're in—wait, are you crying?"

"Yeah," I choke out. "I—I didn't want to bother you. I'm sorry."

"What happened?" she says, instantly serious. "Where are you?"

"I'm back at Onyx. In my apartment." I wipe my nose with the sleeve of my hoodie. "I—Talia, I married him."

"You what?"

"Beckett. After your wedding. I didn't plan it. It just—happened. And I wanted it. We both did."

There's a scramble on her end, Stellan's voice in the background. She's calling him on the line too. "Frankie? Are you okay?"

"No," I whisper. "Not even close."

They listen as I explain everything. The Collettes. The bar. The glass. Beckett walking out with her. How he didn't even look at me.

"Beckett dated Alexandra briefly," Stellan says finally. "In New York. A couple of years ago, maybe more. But he never proposed. I'd bet my life on that. It didn't even last a month. The Collettes... they rewrite reality when it doesn't suit them."

I suck in a breath. "What do you mean?"

"Lorraine Collette's a predator, Frankie. She's been orchestrating social mergers since she was your age. Her first husband was a Vegas tycoon, second was an arms dealer in Monaco, third was some poor bastard from old money Boston. Each one richer than the last."

Talia makes a disgusted noise.

"She groomed her daughter to do the same. Lexi's been her protégé since she could talk. I've seen it—charm, status, public tears. Behind closed doors? She'll twist knives in people's backs just to watch them squirm."

"She slapped me," I whisper. "Then threw a glass at my face. And he didn't even look at me."

Stellan goes quiet for a second. "I'm going to kill him."

"We're coming home," Talia says.

"No. You're on your honeymoon," I say quickly. "Please don't come back. I'm okay."

"You are absolutely not okay," Stellan cuts in firmly.

"I will be," I lie.

"Talk to him," Stellan says gently. "Before this gets messier. Before they spin it even more."

"No." My voice cracks. "I can't. I won't beg someone to care about me."

"We're coming home." Stellan hangs up before I can respond.

"Don't," I plead to dead air. "Please don't. Let me deal with this on my own."

The phone slips from my fingers and thuds against the carpet. I don't bother picking it up.

I press my back to the couch, curling in on myself. My body feels like it's been rung out—like there's nothing left but the ache of being utterly alone.

Because how do you process the kind of pain that isn't physical? The kind that settles into your bones and whispers *you're not enough*?

I gave him everything. I let him see parts of me I've never let anyone near.

And he didn't even look at me.

I clutch a throw pillow to my chest, the fabric soft against the sting on my cheek, still tender from where the glass hit. My blood is on my hoodie. On my skin. And he didn't even flinch.

What hurts more is that I *know* how he looks when he cares.

Today was different. He walked out with someone else.

Chose her lies over my pain.

He didn't even look at me.

My body curls tighter, trembling as I try to catch my breath.

I thought I was done feeling this way.

Thought I'd built walls tall enough, strong enough.

But I let him in.

And now I'm on the floor of my apartment, bleeding and shaking and breaking in a way I haven't since I was eighteen —left, forgotten, too much and never enough all at once.

My ring glints on my finger, and I hate it. I hate how beautiful it is. I hate that I let it mean something.

I twist it once. Twice. Three times.

I don't take it off.

Not yet.

Because as much as I hate him right now—some tiny, splintered part of me still wants it all to have meant something.

Hope is the cruelest feeling—because even after everything, I still have it.

CHAPTER 8
Beckett

LAST NIGHT WAS PROBABLY THE BEST OF MY LIFE.

Frankie and I are finally married—actually married. Not some drunken Vegas technicality. No more pretending, no more secrecy. I can scream her name from rooftops and not feel like she wants to hide.

I slept. Like really slept. Probably because I wasn't up all night thinking about her. She was right beside me.

But when I roll over, the bed is cold.

She's been gone a while.

I throw the covers off and start looking. Maybe she's making breakfast, or curled up with a book.

"Frankie?" I call through the penthouse.

No answer. No note. Nothing.

I check my phone. No text either.

I hate it, but—my mind starts spiraling. What if she regrets it? What if I was the only one who felt it like that?

I call her. Straight to voicemail.

That's the moment I know something's wrong.

I text my assistant.

> I need you to find out where Frankie is.

CLAUDIA

> On it. Give me 5.

Not surprised she's already working. Claudia runs tighter than most machines—more efficient than I'll ever be. I wouldn't survive without her.

CLAUDIA

> She's at The Dutch Wall. Security was dispatched down there. Police were called.

> Why wasn't I informed?

CLAUDIA

> We couldn't get ahold of you. Richard is handling it in his office.

Fucking hell, Frankie. Why didn't you wake me?

I throw on a sweater and jeans, and sprint to the elevator. I call my father while I'm waiting.

He picks up on the first ring like he's expecting me.

"Good morning, son," he says and I can hear the smirk in his voice. "Late night?"

I can't help it. I laugh.

My father and I have always been close. When my mother died, he became my everything. I was sixteen and I couldn't deal with it.

Dad worked full time and mom stayed home with me, I was an only child. She got in the car one day, only to never make it home.

I saw my father fall apart without her, but he picked

68

everything back up for me. It was a main reason why I wanted to take over the Onyx empire.

Onyx was my mother's favorite color. He built this business for her—for us.

"Hi, dad," I say. "What's going on with The Dutch Wall?"

"I got the emergency alert early this morning. Looked like nothing serious at first. Frankie was handling it," he says.

It's what he's not saying that stops me cold. My heart drops to my stomach.

"What are you not telling me?"

"I'm concerned," he says, his voice shifting to a lower tone. "I heard breaking glass and now I've been told law enforcement has been notified."

"I got it, dad," I say. "I know you have some meetings this morning—"

"I want whoever's responsible to be brought to my office," he says. "Let law enforcement meet them here."

"You already know who it is."

"The Collettes," he confirms.

Of course.

That confirms the worst fears I have. They are rabid beasts. When it comes to something they want, they do not ask.

Lorraine gave up on seducing my father a decade ago. Since then, she's been grooming her daughter like bait.

And Lexi's played her part perfectly.

Until now.

"I got it," I say and hang up.

I hear them before I see them—shrill screaming, high and fake. Other voices raised in protest. My pulse spikes.

I start running.

When I reach the bar, all I see is blood.

Frankie. A cut above her eye. Dazed. Standing.

I see red.

She steps toward me, but another figure intercepts—Lexi, with Lorraine behind her like the devil's encore.

My voice is level. "What the hell is going on?"

Lexi spins toward me too fast. Her panic is performative, a role she's memorized down to the microsecond.

"Beckett—finally. She just came at me. She attacked us. Look what she did to my mother. I had to defend us. She did all of this to your bar."

Lorraine clutches her pearls like she's mourning a fallen monarch, not standing in the middle of a luxury bar. The wailing starts a breath later. She cries like it costs her nothing. A parody of grief.

I don't respond. Just watch.

The performance is obvious. But I'm not giving it more stage time.

I cross the distance in three steps, take Lexi firmly by the arm — not rough, just final — and steer her out of the bar without a word. She starts to protest, but I don't stop. I don't slow down. I don't look back.

Let them wail.

"Where are we going?" Lexi stammers, trying to keep up. Lorraine follows, sputtering threats behind us.

Lexi is trying to keep up with me, her mother running behind us. I can barely keep it together. They just screwed with the wrong people.

"We're going to see my father," I say. "You both fucked up."

"But she—"

I cut her off. "I'd shut up if I were you."

We ride up the rest of the way in silence. No one says a word. Then again, I think they're probably scared.

Good. The doors open and I grab Lexi's arm, much to her protest.

I knock and Richard answers before my knuckles can hit the door a second time. "Enter."

He was waiting for us.

I don't like theatrics.

Which is exactly what this has become—Lexi still crying like she's center stage, Lorraine wringing her pearls like we owe her sympathy. I think about the staff standing in place with the kind of stillness that only comes from absolute fear.

Richard looks up from his desk. No smile. No greeting.

"Beckett."

Before I speak, Lorraine lunges for her moment. "Richard —thank god. Your son is—"

"Shut up." I don't think I've ever seen my dad this angry.

Lorraine flinches, but she doesn't drop the act. She adjusts her posture, smooths a hand over her blazer like this is still salvageable. "She's a threat," she says, calm now. "I warned you. We both did."

Lexi doesn't wait. "She attacked me. In your bar. In front of staff. Security. I was defending myself."

"She was bleeding," I say.

That shuts them up for half a second.

"When I got there," I continue, "Frankie was standing still. Lexi was the one yelling. Frankie had a cut on her head and glass with blood on the ground. Since we don't see any marks on you—it's Frankie's blood on that glass."

Lorraine doesn't even blink. "How unfortunate."

Lexi sneers. "She probably did it to herself. That's her game, right? Look helpless. Look wounded. Make men feel guilty enough to protect her. She's a strategist, I'll give her that."

"She's a liar," Lorraine says. "That's how she got here.

71

Built an identity out of performance. Bartender, street smart, emotionally intelligent—please. She's a curated brand, not a real person. She found a weakness and exploited it."

"Your weakness," Lexi adds, smiling now. "All she did was see how badly you wanted someone who didn't care about the Harrington name—and she played that part. Perfectly."

"She doesn't want the name," I say. Feeling like I need to stand up for Frankie.

"She wants what it protects," Lorraine snaps. "The Onyx. The bar. The illusion of power without ever having to pay for it. That's what she's using you for. Legitimacy. She's laundering her ambition through your last name."

Lexi leans forward.

"I've been patient. For years. I've stood beside you when every other woman came and went. I watched you drag yourself through a decade of polite, meaningless proximity. I didn't say a word. I waited. Because I knew. I knew, eventually, you'd remember what legacy looks like when it's done right. And then you threw it away for a woman who thinks gold jewelry and a smoky eye make her untouchable."

Her smile sharpens at the edges. It's actually terrifying how evil it looks.

"She's not untouchable. She's just unguarded. There's a difference. She didn't attack me because she's unhinged," Lexi continues. "She attacked me because I threatened her position. That's all she's holding onto—position. The second you pull your protection, she crumbles."

"She's not a threat because she's dangerous," Lorraine says. "She's a threat because she's clever. And clever, when it's desperate, is fatal."

"People like her always get messy," Lexi finishes. "She's going to slip. She's going to crack. And when she does, the whole thing falls apart. Your name included."

I look at them both. They believe every word. Not because they're hysterical. Not because they're petty.

Because this is how they move. They don't claw their way up—they smile while they push you down.

Frankie didn't just get under their skin—she cut into their future. And they want blood for it.

But they're not getting hers. Not again.

I look to my father. I know his game. His business face. He's thinking about something. Letting them have rope to hang themselves with. I decide to just follow his lead. He is the master businessman afterall.

They pause, like they've said their peace. But of course not, they can't keep their mouths shut to save their lives.

"You remember New York," Lexi says, like it's an important moment that I must remember. "The rooftop in TriBeCa. That night after the Marris auction. We talked until four in the morning about the future. About what it would look like —our names, our families, the kind of influence we could build."

I don't answer.

"You looked at me differently then," she goes on. "Before Vegas pulled you back. Before you got lost in... whatever this is. You and I—we understood each other. You didn't have to explain anything. We just fit."

That's not how I remember it.

We were in TriBeCa for the auction—nothing more. Afterward, we climbed to that rooftop with two other execs and a bottle of stolen champagne she didn't pay for. She talked about influence and merging family powers. Whatever she meant, I didn't care to find out then and I don't care now.

We didn't talk until four. I left before two.

The only thing that stuck with me was her snapping at the bartender for bringing her the wrong drink—twice. Called the intern a liability to his face. Rolling her eyes when the security guard tried to walk us to the car, then made fun of his accent when he left.

She leans in, shoving her chest up, trying to draw as much attention as possible to what she thinks will distract me.

"She doesn't get you, Beckett. Not really. You walk ten steps ahead of everyone else. But I was raised for this. I was shaped for you. You knew it then. And I know you remember it now."

I can't stay quiet anymore. She thinks we were together and I can't have that. "We didn't date, Lexi. We attended the same events. We were photographed in the same cars. And we made the same mistake twice."

Her face cracks for half a second—just a flicker—but she recovers.

"Call it whatever you want. I know what we were. And I know what we could be. If you weren't so busy trying to convince yourself that you and Francine DeLuca somehow belonged together."

Lorraine finally steps in again.

"Lexi makes sense," she says. "And sense matters. Especially in your position. Especially with the eyes on you now. You think Frankie loves you, Beckett? She doesn't even know who you are. But we do. We always have."

Lexi's voice drops to a whisper. "You don't have to be alone in this. Let me in again. Let me help you build what we started."

She looks at me like it's a proposal. Like the answer is already yes.

I look at her like I'm done.

"You were never let in," I say. "You stood next to me and assumed it meant something. You mistook access for closeness."

Lexi swallows hard. "I love you. I've loved you since we were nineteen and you ignored every girl in that room except me. I've waited. I've made myself into everything you need. And I'm not going to watch you throw it away for someone who doesn't understand the first thing about legacy—"

She breathes in, shaky now, eyes locking onto mine.

"—or about you."

Her mother nods once, like this was the moment she'd been waiting for.

"There it is," Lorraine says. "And now you understand why we can't let this stand."

I glance at her. "Let what stand?"

"The infection," she replies.

Lexi exhales. She speaks like she's been holding this in for hours and this is so hard for her. "I didn't want to have to do this."

She pulls out her phone. Taps a folder. Holds the screen up like it's evidence in a trial.

"But since you're still pretending she's some kind of untouchable saint—let's talk about *Francine DeLuca.*"

Lorraine tilts her head, smirking.

"Dr. Carl Hallingsworth," Lexi continues. "Johns Hopkins med school. ER surgeon. Comes from four generations of old-money physicians. Sits on the Harrington-approved list. And, oh—he was supposed to be her husband."

"She never agreed to that," I say flatly.

Lexi smirks. "No? Then why was there a contract?"

My pulse doesn't move. But she feels the shift.

Lorraine speaks next—smooth, surgical.

"The DeLuca-Hallingsworth arrangement wasn't just wishful matchmaking. It was signed. Property tied to it. Silent partner clauses. Backdoor investment in a biotech firm tied to the wedding date. That kind of arrangement."

Lexi nods. "They weren't just planning a wedding. They were consolidating power. And when Frankie decided she was bored? She walked. Tanked the deal. Left Carl to clean up the fallout."

Swipe. Another photo. Hospital hallway. Carl and Frankie mid-argument. Carl's face white-hot. Frankie's lip curled like she's about to punch him.

"She went nuclear," Lexi says. "Started sabotaging his hospital reputation. Got cozy with the board chair's wife. Filed a complaint, then ghosted the follow-up. She left him bleeding—professionally and emotionally. And now you think she's safe to build a future with?"

I don't answer. I want to see how far they'll go.

"She was spoken for, Beckett," Lorraine says coldly. "And you married her knowing she's walked out on empires before."

Lexi stares at me, her voice soft. "She was never yours. Not really. She just made sure you thought you won."

My phone lights up.

Lena.

I'm in the middle of dealing with the Collettes. The last thing I need right now is another interruption.

I answer, trying to stay calm. Although I know my tone comes out more clipped than I intend it too. "What is it?"

"Yes, hi. There's a doctor here harassing Frankie. He grabbed her arm and won't let her leave." Lena's voice is tight. She heard my annoyance and is clearly matching that. "It's Dr. Carl Hallingsworth. He seems to think Frankie doesn't have anyone looking out for her. I thought you'd want to know."

Shit. I'm such an asshole and didn't even bother to ask if she's okay.

76

Suddenly, everything else falls away. Carl's at the hospital, of course he is, he's and ER doctor. But Frankie is there. *Fuck.*

And he put his hands on her. "I'll take care of it."

There's a brief pause, then I can hear the satisfaction in Lena's voice when she responds. "Understood. Thank you, Mr. Harrington."

She hangs up. I'm already pulling up Dr. Kooper's number before the line goes dead.

I don't look at Lexi. Or Lorraine. Not even at my father.

Dr. Kooper answers on the second ring. "This is Kooper." Chief Administrator of St. Avelyn's Medical Center, and the man who's run the place since my mother's final stay.

"This is Beckett Harrington," I say calmly. "Carl Hallingsworth is still employed at your hospital, correct?"

Silence. Then a hesitantly he says, "Yes—he's on a late shift today, I believe. Is there—"

"He put hands on my wife tonight. He refused to let her leave, raised his voice at her in a public hallway. There were witnesses."

A beat. Kooper's voice tightens. "I—hadn't heard that yet, but—"

"You'll hear it in thirty seconds," I cut in. "And you'll fire him in thirty-one. Because what happens if you don't is my family ends our funding. Immediately. No press release. No warning. The new trauma wing you're halfway through building? Gone. The surgical robotics upgrade? Gone. The legacy endowment my mother's name sits on? Gone."

I glance at Richard, checking with him as an afterthought. He doesn't say a word, just nods once.

"Yes, Mr. Harrington. Consider it done."

"I expect confirmation as soon as he's no longer employed there."

Click.

I slide the phone back into my pocket.

Lexi gasps, staring at me opened mouthed.Her games are officially done.

I slide the phone back into my pocket, and look at my father. He speaks, knowing that I'm in no mood to do so.

"Lorraine." She lifts her chin like she still has standing in this room. Richard doesn't break eye contact with her while he speaks. "I allowed you near my family out of respect for your most recent husband. He was a good man. Thoughtful. Loyal. The kind of man who knew the importance of making friends and not enemies."

His tone doesn't change. "You are not that kind of person."

Lorraine freezes. Lexi watches her carefully—like this isn't the first time she's seen her mother be lectured like a child. "I tolerated you," Richard says. "Out of memory. Not merit."

He turns slightly. Just enough to face Lexi, who stiffens like she can feel the floor shifting under her.

"And you," he says. "You benefitted from that same courtesy. You confused inherited proximity with earned relevance. It was never the same thing."

Lexi opens her mouth. He lifts one hand, stopping her words before they could find purchase. "I've watched you posture, play the angles, and try to turn my son into a mark. And tonight you walked into my building, destroyed my property, injured my employee who happens to be my daughter in law, and insulted my son's intelligence."

For the first time, I see the Collettes show fear. My father is not someone to be trifled with. He sits forward, putting his arms on his desk. He is making a promise—removing the final illusion that they belong. "I don't owe you anything."

He turns to me. "Wrap it up."

I look out at the police standing outside and nod for them to come in. They move fast—two of them crossing the room before either woman can adjust their faces.

Lexi startles when the cuffs come out. "What—?"

The officer doesn't blink. "Alexandra Colette, you're being taken into custody on charge of assault."

Lorraine's eyes flash. "You can't be serious. *She's* the one who attacked *us*. That girl—Frankie—she's unstable. Violent. You should be arresting her!"

Lexi tries to twist out of the firm grip, but it's done. Her wrists are already behind her back.

"Beckett," she says, voice trembling with shock. "You're letting them arrest me? You're letting *this* happen?"

"I'm not *letting* anything happen," I say. "I'm ensuring it."

Lorraine steps in, voice rising. "We'll be pressing charges against your wife. Attempted assault. Property damage. Emotional distress."

I raise an eyebrow. "You mean the damage you caused when you tried to corner her in my building? On camera? Surrounded by witnesses?"

Lexi starts to speak, but one of the officers gently guides her toward the exit, cutting her off.Lorraine stays behind just long enough to deliver the parting shot.

"You may have money, Beckett. Power. But women like her don't survive men like you. Not for long."

I give her a bored look, and she gives up, following her daughter out.

I know this isn't over. Not by a longshot.

CHAPTER 9
Beckett

THE ADRENALINE IS GONE NOW, LEAVING THAT hollow, shaken feeling in its place.

"How is Frankie?" My father's question short circuits my brain.

That's when it hits me—I never checked on her.

I walked in, saw the blood on the floor, grabbed Lexi—and just left.

I didn't even ask my wife if she was okay. I'm such a fucking dick. How the fuck could I have done that? "I don't know," I say, dragging both hands over my face. "I didn't check on her."

My dad stares at me like I've grown a second head. "You didn't—what?"

"I didn't think," I admit. "I went in and saw her bleeding... I just... lost it. I wanted to get the Colletts away from her."

He starts to chuckle like he's seen this before. "Shit, son. You have got a lot of grovelling ahead of you. Remember, she needs to be your priority if you want this to work."

"She's probably going to want a divorce now," I say, panic creeping up my spine.

My dad looks at me. His expression shifts—reading me the only way he can. All at once, serious again.

"She loves you, Beckett. She will forgive you—if you earn it. And you will. Marriage is hard. You have to admit when you're wrong and lose your ego."

I nod and turn to find my wife.

"I expect to have dinner with you both sometime soon," he calls after me.

I almost smile. But I'm already putting all of the pieces that my anger shielded me from together. She was in the hospital, she was bleeding and holding her face.

I take off to the penthouse from my father's office. I don't wait a second longer to search for my wife.

Unlocking the door, I go in and look for her. She's nowhere to be found.

Fuck me.

I pull my phone out of my pocket to call her—but it rings first.

Stellan.

What the hell—he's supposed to be on his honeymoon.

I answer immediately. "Why are you calling me? Aren't you in Paris or Tuscany or—"

Talia's voice cuts in, sharp and clear over speaker. "Because your wife went to the ER this morning."

"I know," I mutter. "Lena called me."

Talia's voice lowers, she's pissed. "Why didn't you go with her?"

That question hits like a brick to the sternum.

"I..." I pause. "She was covered in blood, Talia. I didn't know how bad it was—just that Lexi and Lorraine were still in the building, and I needed to neutralize the threat before Frankie walked into more of it."

Silence. No one says it, but it's there. *You chose Colette over your bleeding wife.* It didn't matter why, just that I chose to deal with them rather than my injured wife.

I push forward before they can. "And Carl was there."

Everyone knows about Carl Hallingsworth. He made sure of it. His ego is almost as large as his perceived pedigree. Even more so, we all know about the arrangement that the DeLucas have with the Hallingsworths.

Marriages that are arranged aren't uncommon in this town. Family names are everything.

"What?" Stellan's voice changes. It snaps like a rope with too much tension.

"Hallingsworth," I confirm. "She ran into him at the hospital. Apparently he's working at St. Avelyn's now."

Stellan exhales. I can tell he's holding back restrained rage. "You're kidding me."

"He grabbed her arm. Lena said he wouldn't let her leave. He kept stopping them. At least that's what I'm hearing."

"That son of a—" Stellan doesn't finish the sentence. "They arranged that match when she was what—nineteen?"

"Lexi used him as ammo," I say. "Said Frankie went from his bed to mine. Tried to paint her like some kind of status chasing queen."

Stellan's quiet for a second. "Did you handle Hallingsworth? If not, I will. The asshole deserves it."

"I got him fired within ten minutes. Called Dr. Kooper myself. Told him either Carl walked or the Harringtons pulled every dollar from that hospital."

I should've been there. Not cleaning up after the mess those two women created. If I just stopped to think about what I needed for just a second, Hallingsworth would've never had the opportunity to get close to her.

"Good," Stellan mutters.

"And as for the Colette circus—" I drag a hand through my hair—"I didn't think. I just saw the blood, saw Frankie's face, and everything went dark. I pulled them out of the Wall and straight to my father's office. Got the police to meet us there. Pressed charges on Lexi for assault."

"About time."

"But I should've gone to Frankie first." I admit it. I have to. "I needed to walk out with her and not Lexi. She must think I didn't fight for her."

"She didn't need to see you fight for her, Beckett," Talia says. "She needed to see you *show up*."

I nod. "I'm going to find her now."

"We're coming home," Talia says, adamantly.

I rub the back of my neck. "You don't have to do that."

"We know," she replies. "But we're doing it anyway."

"You're on your honeymoon." I cannot have fucked up this badly. Enough for them to leave their honeymoon early. Panic is clawing its way up my throat. *What did I do?*

"Yeah," Stellan says. "And Carl Hallingsworth just put his hands on your wife in a public ER. Lexi's pressing false charges, trying to ruin Frankie's credibility. You really think this is something we watch unfold from a vineyard in Tuscany?"

I don't answer.

Talia doesn't wait. "We're not just coming back for Frankie. We're coming back for both of you. Because this isn't over."

"I'm handling it."

"Lexi's not going to stop," Talia says. "You embarrassed

her. Had her arrested. She's not just hurt. She's humiliated. And she's dangerous when she's cornered."

"She already used Carl like a weapon," I say. "She threw him and Frankie at me like it would actually make me change my mind about being married to her. Thought it'd make her look cheap. Or unstable at least."

"She knew exactly what she was doing," Stellan mutters. "Your wife's history is her ammunition now."

"He's done. Fired. He has no reason to ever go near her again."

"Don't be naïve," he says flatly. "Carl's a loose end. Rothwell security flagged him last year. He's got unreported connections —intel firms, a lobby group in D.C., offshore encrypted accounts. He's a narcissist with ambition and something to prove."

"Jesus," I mutter.

"And," Talia adds, "he's obsessed with appearances. The perfect match, the perfect life. She humiliated him. He's not going to let that go."

What do I do now? Stellan is the best at this. Talia is too.

"We may need to call in Opal," Talia says.

That's probably the last thing I expected any of them to say and the last person I want to help us.

"No," I say, immediately.

Stellan's voice hardens. "Absolutely not."

"She's already been briefed," Talia says. "Just eyes-on. No engagement. She's still in Vegas. She never left."

"You're serious?" I ask. "Opal?"

"She's embedding with the Shadow Brides, trying to reestablish trust," Talia explains. "And she wants to help."

"She nearly collapsed Strategic," Stellan snaps. "She walked out on protocol, burned every outpost we had in Berlin, and handed our enemies a blueprint in the process."

"She thought she was protecting someone who couldn't protect themselves," Talia replies quietly.

"And she dismantled everything we built to do it," he counters. "She betrayed you, Talia. Or did you forget that part?"

"I didn't forget anything," she says. "I also didn't forget how fast she moved when I told her Frankie was in danger."

"You told her?" My tone is deadly. Talia crossed a line. "This is my wife. I don't want that woman anywhere near her."

"She has access we don't," Talia says. "And if half of what she found is true, we need all of the information. Now."

I glance toward the window, tension anchoring my spine.

"You trust her?"

Talia doesn't answer right away. "I trust that she won't act without consent. I trust that she regrets what she did. And I trust that if she wanted to hurt us again—she wouldn't be asking for permission."

"She doesn't speak to Frankie," Stellan says, his voice hard in a way that I can appreciate. "She doesn't breathe in her direction. She stays hidden behind the scenes."

"Agreed," I say. "One wrong move, and she's done."

Talia exhales. "She won't screw this up. And she sure as shit won't *attack* her."

Ouch. Okay, I deserved that.

"She better not," Stellan mutters. "Because if she does—she won't get a third chance."

I pause, jaw locked. "We're really doing this?"

"We are," Talia confirms. "Private jet leaves in fifteen. We'll land before sunrise."

I shut my eyes. "Okay."

"Make sure she's somewhere safe," Talia adds. "And Beckett? Don't wait too long to find her and apologize."

The phone clicks as Stellan hangs up.

I don't need to ask where she is.

She's not at the hospital anymore. She's not hiding out at The Dutch Wall. And she sure as hell isn't anywhere near my penthouse.

There's only one place she'd go—her apartment.

The one that still smells like her shampoo and overpriced candles. And probably mildew at this point. But still, it's more of a home than mine is.

I take the private elevator. Last thing I need is to be interrupted by someone that wants to talk.

The door's unlocked.

I push it open as quietly as possible. Just in case she is sleeping or something.

She's on the couch, curled up in one of my hoodies, legs pulled to her chest, hair wet, bandage at her temple. No TV. No music.

Her eyes are open, fixed on nothing.

I step inside, shut the door behind me.

She knows I'm here. The way her spine straightens slightly. The way her fingers grip the blanket a little tighter.

Earlier today, she was looking at me like I was the safest place in the world.

And now she won't look at me at all.

CHAPTER 10

Frankie

HE'S HERE. HE CAME. BUT IT DOESN'T MATTER AT THIS point.

He wasn't there when it counted. He wasn't there while the blood was pouring down my face, when my hands were shaking so hard I couldn't even move. Not even when I had to hold a towel to my head and wait for someone to come give me stitches.

Now he's in my apartment, watching me, probably trying to figure out how to fix this.

But I'm not a problem to be solved.

I'm the person he was supposed to love—supposed to put first. And he didn't.

He showed up for her first. He's here, but it's too little too late.

"I handled the wrong thing first," Beckett says, voice low and tight. His teeth clenched and jaw tight.

Of course he did. Congratulations. Gold star for awareness.

He steps a little closer, not enough to crowd me, but enough that I can feel the weight of him trying to fix it.

"I saw you bleeding," he continues, like that's some kind of excuse. "And all I could think about was punishment. Making them pay. Getting them out. I thought if I moved fast enough, you'd be safe."

I don't look at him. I'm not sure if it's because I don't want to, or I simply can't yet.

"But I left you there," he says. "I didn't check. I didn't ask if you could stand. I just—reacted."

Yeah. He reacted alright—to everything but me.

"I should've seen you first," he goes on. "Should've walked straight to you, made sure you were okay. Taken you to the ER myself. Sat there with you, held your hand, demanded every test in the damn hospital—"

He's still talking, and not a single word is making it past the wall in my head.

"I just thought—I thought I had to get Lexi out before she did more damage. That if I handled it fast enough, I could get back to you and—"

God. He won't shut up.

I count his excuses like minutes ticking off a clock.

One. Two. Three. Four.

Still talking.

Still spinning out this little redemptive monologue like it's going to bring us back together.

I stare at the blanket in my lap, tracing the stitching with my pointer finger. Thinking about how I'd rather chew glass than sit through one more explanation of how his feelings *overwhelmed him*.

"I wasn't trying to hurt you," he says. "I swear, Frankie, if I could go back—"

I sigh loudly, just to see if he notices.

He doesn't.

"And I know it doesn't mean much now, but I haven't

stopped thinking about it. About you. About how I made you feel—" Suddenly, his voice changes, sharpens. "Are you listening?"

I look up, slowly. When my gaze meets his deep brown eyes, my patience snaps like a thread pulled too tight. "Don't ask me that," I say, my voice deceptively quiet.

His brows shoot up his forehead.

"I'm listening," I bite. "I've been listening. To every damn word coming out of your mouth since you walked in here with your guilty eyes and your broken record apologies."

He tries to speak, but I raise my hand to stop him.

"And it doesn't matter. Because you're still doing it, Beckett. You're still centering your guilt. Your reaction. Your pain. Not once have you asked what it felt like to be left there. Not once have you said the words I'm actually waiting for."

He opens his mouth again. I don't let him get a word out.

"I needed you," I say. "And you made the choice to see to Lexi Collette first."

His mouth parts like he might argue. I stand slowly, the blanket falling off my legs. I don't bother adjusting his hoodie. Let him see the bandage on my cheek. Exactly what he wasn't there for.

"I need space," I say, holding my chin high.

His throat works like he's trying to swallow it down.

"I just... I need time to breathe," I add, my voice goes thin. I'm about to snap. "To think without you hovering. I need a second to stop the pain I feel before I start forgiving."

His face falls, but he nods.

"I'll go," he says.

I walk to the door and open it, not looking back. When he steps past me, I don't stop him.

I just close the door.

This time, I lock it.

I let all of the air out of my lungs. It feels like I've been holding it all night.

I move on autopilot. One light off. Then another. The lamp by the window hums for half a second before it dies, leaving me in that in-between gray that only exists in expensive apartments after midnight. The city glows faintly through the glass—soft blues and pinks bleeding across the skyline like bruises.

It's beautiful. I hate it for being beautiful.

I walk barefoot across the cold tile, feeling the sting with every step. It grounds me. Reminds me that I still exist outside of whatever's happening in my head. The hoodie hangs heavy on my shoulders, the fabric thick and warm, smelling faintly of his cologne—cedar, amber, something that could have meant *home*.

Every inch of my body aches—not from the cut on my head or the bruises blooming under my skin— from something marrow deep that chills me to the core.

Heartbreak.

The bathroom light is too bright when I flip it on. My reflection looks worse than I expect. Mascara smudged around bloodshot eyes, bruises coming to life in a random pattern.

I brush my teeth. I need something normal to do, something to keep my hands busy. The mint burns, my throat tastes like metal. I rinse, spit, then stare at myself until I can't stand it anymore.

I pull the sweatshirt tighter around me, tucking my hands into the sleeves until my fingers disappear. I climb into bed without turning down the covers, curling up like I used to as a kid when the house got too loud.

The sheets are cool against my legs. But my heart won't stop racing, like it's bracing for another blow.

I turn to my side, facing the wall. The blanket scratches at my skin. His hoodie clings to me, still damp around the cuffs from where I gripped it too hard.

I bury my face into the pillow and squeeze my eyes shut.

I hate this. All the pain. I hid myself from that for years. Blocked myself from the possibility of getting hurt.

I shouldn't have let it get to me. I'm better than that.

But Lexi's lies, Lorraine's smug little act, Beckett's indifference beat like a drum inside of my head.

His excuses crawled under my skin and burrowed deep into my soul. I have spent years building armor to survive people like them, just for them to wipe it away in a millisecond.

I press my knuckles to my ribs, like I can shove the ache back in.

I'm not supposed to break like this. Not over people like that. I know better.

And yet—I still feel like I'm eighteen again, left outside a closed door, waiting to be chosen.

I thought Beckett would be different this time.

He's my husband, my choice. Not only that, he chose me, too.

I choke on a breath and shove the blanket into my mouth so I won't make a sound. My tears slip out anyway. I taste salt on my tongue and feel my face twist as I try to keep it in. But it's no use, I can't. Not tonight.

I cry harder, not because of the Collettes or the mess at The Wall or the blood on the floor.

I cry because I hate how much I care.

Because I don't know what I need from him now—or if anything he says could even fix it.

Even though part of me still wants him to try.

And that part feels like betrayal.

I curl in tighter, like I'm trying to fold myself so small that I blink out of existence. My jaw locks. My breath stutters. Every part of me feels wrung out—eyes raw, limbs sore, chest like it's been scooped out and left hollow. My fingers dig into the mattress, just to feel something solid. Something that won't leave.

I cry until I can't breathe through my nose.

Until my throat burns and the pillow is damp and I'm not even sure what I'm crying for anymore—him or me.

I cry because I feel weak.

I know I'm not.

Not really.

But God, tonight, I feel like it.

Sleep doesn't take me gently. It drags me under—face still wet, hoodie too warm, heart still cracked open in the dark.

I don't know what's waiting for me in the morning.

Only that I won't be the same again.

I squint my eyes as the morning light blinks through the blinds, the sound of pounding in the distance wakes me.

The light stings. My lashes stick together as I crack my eyes open.

I blink hard, but the pillow's wet. My cheek is clammy where it pressed into the soaked cotton.

I shift. My spine protests. So do my knees. I must've curled in too tight. The ache feels earned.

I sit up slow, like every inch of me weighs double. The blanket slides down my arms. My skin is cold underneath.

There's a pull at my temple—the bandage tugging just enough to remind me I'm not fine.

I swing my legs over the edge of the bed. The floor is freezing. I flinch, but don't pull back.

The knocking is increasing in speed. I check the clock on the microwave. 6AM.

"Who is it?" My voice is a barely audible croak.

I look through the doorbell camera and see Talia waving on the other side. Her chestnut hair braided on the side of her head. Brown eyes smiling at me. She's holding coffee. Two of them.

She looks too stiff for someone who just got back from her honeymoon.

I throw the door open and hug her as tight as I can. I've missed her. Since she walked into our lives, she's become one of my closest friends. Though, I did have to push a bit at first.

"You look like shit," she says softly.

"Thanks. You really know how to comfort a girl."

She smiles. But only for a second. "Can I come in?"

I step back and let her in. The silence stretches as I shut the door. I feel like I should say something, but I don't. I just wrap both hands around the coffee cup and try not to let it burn a hole through me.

Talia moves to the couch and sits like she's been here a thousand times and makes herself comfortable.

"You slept in it," she says, nodding toward the hoodie.

I look at the worn, black fabric, lifting my hand to inspect the cuff dangling off. "I didn't mean to."

"But you did."

I sit down beside her. Far enough away where I can keep some space between us, but close enough where I don't feel so alone.

She waits, just like she always does, until I'm ready to talk.

"I feel stupid," I say finally. "I let my wall down. I let myself believe he—"

"He what?" She cuts me off. The look on her face tells me that I'm missing some point she's trying to make.

"Would put me first."

She doesn't say anything. Just takes a sip of her coffee and waits again.

"I feel weak," I admit. "Like I should've known better. Should've seen it coming. The second I let myself believe, it all collapsed."

"You think loving someone is weak?"

"No," I say, too quickly. "But I think expecting someone to choose you—that's where I messed up."

Talia looks at me like she's not taking anymore shit from me. "He did choose you, Frankie. He married you. He went nuclear on the Collettes. He got Lexi and her mother arrested."

"And he left me bleeding in a bar."

"Because he was too busy making sure you wouldn't be bleeding worse." She doesn't snap at me, but it feels like a slap to the face. Truth without malice. Her tone is soft, though. She's trying to soften the blow.

I flinch. Her eyes turn soft.

"Look, I'm not saying he got it perfect. God knows he didn't. I've always been good at reading people, at seeing their true feelings. And I know the way he looks at you scares the shit out of him."

My throat tightens.

"He loves you, Frankie. You want to be mad at him? Be mad. You want space? Take it. But don't twist it into a story where you were the only one who fell."

I stare down at my coffee.

She leans forward. "That man has never looked at another

woman the way he looks at you. Not even close. You think your wall crumbled? His never existed when it came to you."

I look up at her.

"Just give him a chance to heal what he broke because you know he will never stop trying."

She's right. I do know that. He won't. So maybe I should let him explain instead of shutting myself off to him.

I blow out a breath and let my head fall to the back of the couch, wincing when it shoots pain through my injuries. "I'll text him."

I pull out my phone.

> I'm ready. Whenever you are.

The reply comes almost immediately.

BECKETT

> I can be there in 10.

> I'll be here.

"He coming?" She smirks and hops up.

"Yeah," I say. "We can work this out."

"I know you can, Franks," she says, turning to leave. "I believe you both deserve love."

She is one to speak.

She found love.

The kind that didn't come easy.

The kind that nearly broke them both.

Now I get it.

If Beckett and I want any chance at all—we'll have to fight like hell to earn it.

CHAPTER 11

Frankie

I WAIT FOR BECKETT BY MYSELF. THE THOUGHTS rushing through my head won't stop.

What if this doesn't work? What if I can't get past it? What if he says all the right things and I still feel this hollow ache in my chest?

What if I'm not strong enough to let him back in?

I pace the length of my apartment—kitchen to living room, living room to bedroom, bedroom back to kitchen. The coffee Talia brought sits cold on the counter. I haven't touched it since she walked in. Even though it's my favorite, I just can't bring myself to drink it.

My phone lights up.

BECKETT

I'm here.

My stomach drops. I wasn't ready five minutes ago. I'm definitely not ready now.

But I walk to the door anyway, unlock it, and pull it open.

He's standing there looking destroyed. Hair a mess. Eyes

bloodshot. Still wearing the same clothes from yesterday—jeans rumpled, and sweater wrinkled like he never took them off.

He's holding two fresh coffees and a bag from the bakery I love. The one I mentioned once, months ago, when we were still pretending we didn't want each other. Before we ever said I do.

"Hi," he says quietly.

"Hi."

We stand there. Neither of us moving.

"Can I come in?" he asks.

I step aside without a word.

He walks past me, sets the coffee and bag on the counter with careful precision. Like if he moves too fast, I'll disappear. Then he turns to face me, hands shoved deep in his pockets.

"I brought breakfast," he says. "Wasn't sure if you'd eaten."

"I haven't."

He nods. Opens his mouth. Closes it. Tries again.

"Frankie, I—" He stops, exhales hard, drags a hand through his already messy hair. "I fucked up. I know I did. And I need you to let me explain."

"So explain."

He winces. Like he was hoping I'd make this easier. Maybe meet him with some sympathy, but that won't be happening.

When he realizes that, he takes a breath and starts talking. "When I walked into that bar and saw you bleeding—"

"Stop."

He freezes.

I shake my head. "Talia already explained it. The whole 'you went into protect mode' thing. How you needed to eliminate the threat. I get it."

"Then why—"

"Because understanding it doesn't make it hurt less," I cut him off. My tone portrays all of the frustration I'm feeling inside. "I don't need you to explain your thought process, Beckett. I need you to understand what it felt like to be left there."

His jaw works. He looks like I just punched him in the gut.

Good.

"I needed you," I say, and my voice cracks despite my best effort. "Not ten minutes later. Not after you handled Lexi. I needed you *then*. And you walked right past me."

"Frankie—"

"You didn't even look at me." The words come out jagged. "There was blood on my face and you didn't even *look* at me."

He takes a step forward. I take one back.

"Don't," I warn.

He stops. Hands still in his pockets. Looking at me like I'm breaking him.

"You're right," he says quietly. "You're absolutely right."

I look away, towards the window and the city light blurring on the other side.

"I should've come to you first," he continues, voice tight. "The second I walked in and saw you bleeding, I should've pushed everyone else aside and made sure you were okay."

"But you didn't."

"No. I didn't." He takes a breath. "And I will regret that for the rest of my life."

I nod slowly. He's not wrong.

"Frankie, I need you to know—I wasn't thinking. I saw you hurt and something in me just... snapped. All I could think about was making them pay. Getting them out. I thought if I moved fast enough, you'd be safe."

"I needed you," I say quietly, my throat tightening. "Do you know what it felt like? Standing there while you walked away with her?"

"I'm so sorry—"

"I don't want sorry." I finally turn to face him. "I want you to understand. Lena and Roxy took me to the hospital. *They* sat with me. *They* held my hand while I got stitches. *They* advocated for me. *They* cared for me."

His face crumples, the heartbreak and regret are evident in the shift in his eyes.

"And the whole time," I continue, voice shaking now, "I kept thinking maybe you'd show up. Maybe you'd come through those doors and—" I stop. Swallow hard. "But you didn't."

"I should have."

"Yes, you should have. I don't know how to get past this," I admit. "I don't know how to trust that I come first when you made it abundantly clear that I don't."

"Tell me what you need," he says quietly. "Tell me how to fix this."

"I don't know if you can." I don't know if it's my words, or the way that I say them, but that landed hard. I watch him absorbing it, to the best of his abilities that is.

"But I want to try," I add, softer now. "I just... I need to know you understand. That you won't do this again."

"I won't," he says immediately, reaching his hand out to touch me, maybe grab my hand, I'm not sure, but I don't give him the chance to make contact, not yet. "I swear to you, Frankie, I will never—"

"You can't promise that," I interrupt gently. "You can't know what you'll do in the moment. What you can promise is to try."

He nods, throat working.

"I love you," I whisper. "But what you did yesterday was devastating."

"I know." His voice breaks. "I'm so sorry. I'm so fucking sorry."

I stare at him. At the mess he's become—red eyes, rumpled everything, hands that won't stop shaking. He looks like shit, in some twisted way, I'm glad. I'm glad I'm not the only one.

But something shifts when I look at him standing there, wrecked and desperate in the middle of my apartment.

I've spent years building walls. Brick by brick. Every time someone left, every time I wasn't chosen, every time I was told I was too much or not enough—I added another layer. I made myself harder to reach, harder to hurt. But no one knew. Of course, I was happy, laughing. I wore a layer of armour that radiated joy and warmth, without ever truly letting anyone in.

I don't want to do this alone anymore.

The thought terrifies me because wanting someone means they can hurt you, they can walk away. Beckett did that. Loving someone comes with risk and pain and standing in a bar with blood on my face wondering why I wasn't enough. He showed me that.

But he came back. Showed up at seven in the morning looking like he hasn't slept, like the thought of losing me is killing him. He's standing in my apartment ready to beg, to grovel, to get on his knees if I asked him to. That has to mean something.

I don't want to build walls anymore. I don't want to protect myself so hard that I lose the one person who actually fought to stay, who showed up even when I told him to leave, who's still here even though I haven't forgiven him yet.

He fucked up horribly. But he knows it, and he's here now

willing to do whatever it takes. And I'm exhausted from being angry, from holding everything so tight that I can't breathe. I've been so angry at him for so long. I can't do it anymore, he's proven himself, hasn't he?

Letting him in again—really in—terrifies me. But I'm tired of being safe and alone. I'm tired of the walls.

I take a breath and feel them start to crack, start to crumble.

It's terrifying, but I'm doing it anyway.

He doesn't say anything. Just watches me like I'm a puzzle he's trying to solve, giving me the chance to walk away.

But I'm not walking away.

One step, then another. My heart's pounding so hard I can feel it in my throat, slamming against my ribs like it's trying to beat me to him.

Beckett doesn't move until I'm right in front of him— close enough to smell his cologne, that clean, expensive scent that always makes my stomach flip. His hands stay at his sides. His jaw is tight. His eyes won't leave my face.

Something inside me snaps.

I grab his shirt, fist the fabric hard, and pull.

His body collides with mine—solid, warm, tense like he's been waiting, willing me to do this. My mouth crashes into his. It's not gentle. It's not sweet. It's every silent argument, every ache, every time I watched him walk away when I wanted him to stay.

He staggers back a step. I go with him, pushing until his back hits the wall. I press into him—hips, chest, mouth—all of it.

He groans, low and rough, and that sound shoots straight through me.

His hands are on me now. One gripping my waist, the

other sliding up my back, fingers threading into my hair like he's afraid I'll vanish if he lets go.

I bite his bottom lip—just enough to make a point—and he growls.

"Thank God," he mutters against my lips like a prayer.

He kisses me back like he means it.

The air between us is hot. My pulse is racing. His hands slide under my shirt, dragging heat across skin that's already trembling.

I want him. Now. I want to feel him lose control. I want to destroy whatever distance is left between us.

I break the kiss long enough to catch my breath. Press my lips to his jaw, trail them to the corner of his mouth.

"No more walls," I tell him. "No more holding back."

"Let me in," he's begging me "All the way. I'm not going anywhere."

CHAPTER 12

Beckett

I KISS HER BEFORE SHE CAN CHANGE HER MIND.

Not rough. Not soft either. Just honest. Everything I've been holding back, poured into her mouth like a promise I don't know how to say out loud.

She doesn't pull away. Doesn't hesitate. Her hands grip the sides of my shirt like she's been waiting for this longer than I have.

I press her back until her spine touches the wall. My mouth moves against hers.

She tilts her head and opens for me.

Every part of me aches with how much I want her. Not just her body—though, fuck, that too—but the way she's letting me in. She isn't hiding behind armour or sarcasm.

I slide my hand into her hair and tilt her head so I can taste deeper. Her breath hitches. Her body leans into mine like she's all in now. No more second guessing. No more playing safe.

I pull back just enough to speak against her lips. "Say it again."

Her eyes flicker up to mine, already heavy with heat. "No more walls."

That's all I need.

I lift her without thinking. Her legs wrap around my waist like muscle memory. Her mouth is on my throat now, hot and frantic. My hands grip her thighs, holding her tight as I walk us to the bedroom.

The door gives with a bump against the wall. I don't stop moving. She pulls me back down with both hands fisted in my shirt.

So I give her everything. Every single part of me, all through our bodies,through my lips on hers, through everything.

I tug the sweatshirt over her head and toss it somewhere behind me, not caring where it lands. All I can see is her— bare skin, flushed and rising with each breath.

Her bra follows—black, lacy, and barely there to begin with. Her breasts spill free like the best gift in the entire world, and for a second, I just look.

She's beautiful in the way that makes everything else disappear. She's letting me see her. Not just like this, naked and arched beneath my hands, but real. With no shield up and a smile just for me.

Her nipples are already tight, and I don't stop myself from brushing my thumb across one. Just to feel her. Just to see her react. Her breath hitches and it does something to me. I want to possess her. Fully and completely.

She doesn't flinch, she leans into it.

God, the way her body responds like it knows mine. The way my hands fit against her curves like they were built with her in mind. She's not just desire. She's gravity.

Right now, all I want is to worship the very ground she walks on.

Frankie watches me like she's burning—eyes glassy, lips parted, skin flushed. She drags her hands down her own stomach, teasing, tempting, knowing exactly what that does to me.

I see her bare thighs and a flash of black lace teasing beneath the hem. She's soaked through the black lace of her panties.

I reach for the hem and slide it down painfully slow. I want to savor every moment with her. She lifts her hips to help me, eyes locked on mine like she wants me to *feel* how badly she wants this.

My heart thuds like a war drum in my chest.

I groan, low and rough. "You want me to take my time, or make you come fast first?"

"Both. But start with the second."

Christ. I drag her panties off and spread her thighs. The heat of her hits me like a punch.

I kiss up one thigh, then the other, until she squirms.

"Beckett—"

I bury my mouth between her legs.

She gasps, one hand fisting in my hair, the other grabbing the sheets. I lap at her slowly, letting her feel every stroke of my tongue.

She tastes like heat and home. Like something I'll never get enough of.

When I slide two fingers inside her, she arches up. "Fuck —yes—"

She's tight and warm and perfect, already pulsing around me.

"I need you inside me," she gasps. "Now."

I move up her body and kiss her hard, letting her taste herself on my mouth.

"Turn over."

Her breath catches. But she obeys.

On her knees, hands braced on the headboard, she looks over her shoulder at me— absolutely perfect with hair messy, eyes molten.

"You gonna make me beg for it?"

I grip her hips. "You already did."

With one slow thrust, she moans. Her back arches, pressing her hips into mine.

The sound that leaves her is pure surrender, torn from somewhere deep inside her. Her body curves back into me, trembling with the effort of holding on and letting go at the same time. I feel her breath falter, her thighs tighten where they cradle me. She's giving me everything, right now,

She takes me fully, her body stretching around me with a heat that steals my balance. She's so tight, the pressure surrounding me is near unbearable, like her body is trying to memorize every inch of mine—take it in, hold it there, never let go. The heat of her pussy, the way she grips me as I push deep—it's visceral. I can feel her everywhere, not just around me but pulling me deeper, pulsing with need.

The sensation crashes through my spine in waves. My muscles lock, trying to keep pace with the way she's taking me. She doesn't resist—she yields. She doesn't hide it. Doesn't try to bite it back. She just feels it. All of it.

"More," she gasps. "Harder."

But I don't give it to her. Not yet.

I slow down. Every stroke is deep and dragging, designed to make her feel it. To make her *need* it. Her fingers grip the headboard so tightly her knuckles go white, and she pushes her hips back into mine with a soft sound.

"Beckett," she pants. "Please—"

God, the sound of her begging, the way her body trembles

under my hands—it's enough to make my control slip. But I hold the line. Just a little longer.

"Show me how much you want it," I growl against her shoulder, my hand splaying across her lower back, holding her still.

She moves for me. Hips rolling. Body opening. A gasp falling from her lips every time I push back in. She's so wet, so tight, taking me deeper each time, like her body's built to handle all of me.

Her thighs start to shake. She's right on the edge.

That's when I give it to her.

I snap my hips forward. Faster. Rougher. Every thrust punches a breath from her lungs. Her raw, strangled cries fill the room.

I reach around and find her clit, slick and swollen. My fingers circle tight and relentless as she jerks, a sob catching in her throat.

"That's it," I growl. "Come for me. Let go."

She shatters.

Her body clamps down around me, pulsing hard and fast. I follow her over the edge, burying myself deep, groaning her name like a prayer.

We collapse in a tangled, panting heap.

She rolls onto her side and looks at me, cheeks flushed, hair wild.

"Well," she says, trying to catch her breath. "That was one way to apologize."

I laugh. "You're the one who attacked me."

"Attacked is a strong word."

"You shoved me against a wall."

"You didn't seem to mind." She traces a lazy finger down my chest.

"I definitely didn't mind."

"Good. Because I'm still a little mad at you." She's grinning though.

"A *little* mad?"

"Maybe seventy-five percent forgiven."

"Seventy-five?" I raise an eyebrow. "What do I have to do for the other twenty-five?"

She pretends to think about it. "Food. I'm starving."

"I brought you breakfast."

"It's cold now." Her pouting face makes me groan again. She's perfect, there is absolutely nothing in this world that I wouldn't give her.

"Whose fault is that?"

She smacks my chest. "Yours for being distracting."

"Me? You grabbed *my* shirt." I feign indignation, smiling a smile that's more real than any before.

"You were standing there all sad and pretty. What was I supposed to do?"

"Sad and pretty?"

"Don't let it go to your head." But she's smiling.

I pull her closer. "Too late."

She laughs, warm and satisfied against my chest. For a moment, we just lie there—her pressed against me, my hand sliding up and down her spine.

"Come on," I say finally, kissing the top of her head. "Let's go eat breakfast. I've been trying to feed you for hours," I flick her nose gently. "You're the one who kept getting distracted."

"Pretty sure that was mutual."

"Fair." I sit up, taking her with me. "But I'm not letting you pass out from hunger. That would be bad husband protocol."

She rolls her eyes but she's smiling. "Fine. But I'm wearing your hoodie."

"Deal."

She pulls it on—drowning in it, looking absolutely perfect —and I grab my sweater from wherever she threw it earlier.

"Beckett?" she says as I open the door.

I turn back.

Her expression softens. "Thank you. For fighting for us."

My chest tightens. "Always."

She takes my hand, lacing our fingers together.

This is what I wanted all along. It just took a minute for us to get there.

CHAPTER 13
Frankie

WE END UP AT BECKETT'S PLACE BECAUSE, ACCORDING to him, my kitchen is tragically understocked.

"I have food," I argue as we step into the elevator.

"You have hot sauce and coffee." He gives me a deadpan look that makes me laugh.

"I have the essentials, you know."

He shakes his head, but he's smiling. His hand hasn't left mine since we walked out of my apartment.

I'm not complaining.

The doors open and he pulls me toward his front door. The penthouse feels different now. Less like his space and more like... ours? That's terrifying and comforting at the same time.

"Sit," he says, guiding me toward the kitchen island. "I'll cook."

"You cook?"

"Don't sound so surprised."

"I've literally never seen you cook."

"That's because you've spent more time avoiding me than being with me," he points out, pulling eggs and vegetables from the fridge.

Fair.

I watch him move around the kitchen—efficient, confident, sleeves rolled up to his elbows. It's unfairly attractive.

"Stop staring," he says without looking up.

"I'm not staring." Oh, I'm *definitely* staring.

"You absolutely are."

"Maybe I'm just hungry." I shrug, a small smile pulling at my lips again. This man, he's mine and God, I'm happy.

"Sure." But he's grinning.

I prop my chin in my hand. "So what are you making, Chef Harrington?"

"Omelets. Nothing fancy."

"I'm impressed you know how to crack an egg."

"I like cooking." He whisks the eggs with more skill than I expected. "My mom taught me."

That stops me. He rarely talks about her.

"Yeah?" I say softly.

"Yeah. She said I needed to know how to take care of myself. And anyone I loved." He pours the eggs into the pan. "She'd like you, I think."

My throat tightens. "You think?"

"She'd love how you don't take my shit." He smiles, but there's sadness in it. "She never did either."

I don't know what to say to that. So I just reach across the counter and squeeze his hand.

He squeezes back just as the door opens. We both freeze.

"You expecting someone?" I ask, making to stand.

"No—" He stops. "Shit. My dad has a key."

"Your dad has a—"

"Beckett?" Richard's voice echoes through the penthouse. "You home?"

Beckett looks at me, slightly panicked. "I forgot he said he might stop by this morning."

"It's fine," I whisper.

"You sure?"

I nod. Even though I'm suddenly very aware that I'm wearing Beckett's hoodie, no bra, and my hair is definitely sex hair.

Richard rounds the corner and stops when he sees me. "Frankie," he says, surprised but smiling. "I didn't know you were here. But I'm glad you are."

"Hi, Richard." I try to look casual. Like I always hang out at his son's place at ten in the morning looking thoroughly kissed. We are married after all.

His eyes flick between us—noting the domesticity of the scene, the way Beckett's still holding a spatula, my hand on the counter close to his.

"Am I interrupting?" He asks, but there's a knowing glint in his eye.

"No," Beckett says quickly. "I'm making breakfast. Want some?"

Richard looks at me, then at Beckett, then back to me. A slow smile spreads across his face.

"I'd love some," he says, pulling out a stool next to me.

Beckett shoots me an apologetic look. I shrug. Honestly, if anyone is going to walk in on us, Richard's not the worst option.

"Coffee?" Beckett offers.

"Please."

I watch Beckett move around the kitchen, pouring coffee, flipping the omelet with practiced ease. Richard watches too, but his attention keeps drifting to me.

"So," Richard says casually. "You two seem... good."

I nearly choke on my coffee. "Uh. Yeah. We're good."

"Good." He nods like he's confirming something to himself. "That makes me happy."

"How's the bar?" Richard asks.

"Recovering," I say honestly. "We're getting the damage cleaned up. Should be fully operational by tonight."

His expression darkens slightly. "I'm still furious about what the Collettes did to you."

"Yeah. Me too." A humorless laugh pushes it's way through me

"They won't be bothering you again," he says firmly. "I made sure of that."

"Thank you. For having my back."

"Always, Frankie. You're part of this family—whether you married my son or not." He pauses. "Though I'm glad you did."

Beckett's ears turn red. "Dad—"

He puts the omelet in front of me and kisses the top of my head before sliding another one in front of Richard.

"What? I'm just relieved you finally did something about it." Richard takes a bite of his omelet. "Do you know how many times over the years he's asked me about you? How's Frankie doing? Is she happy at the bar? Did she mention me?"

"Dad, stop," Beckett warns.

"Oh, and my personal favorite," the mischievous glint in his eyes has me grinning, there's no one that's been able to get under Beckett's skin like his father. "when you were in New York and you asked me to promote her to general manager because, and I quote, 'she's the most competent person we have and she deserves it.'"

I turn to look at Beckett. "You did that?"

"It was a business decision," he mutters.

"Was it a business decision when you had me send her flowers every year on her birthday?" Richard asks innocently.

"Anonymously, of course, because God forbid she knew they were from you."

My jaw drops. "The flowers were from you?"

Beckett won't look at me. "Dad, I swear—"

"And let's not forget the time you redesigned the entire staff apartment building because you said, and I'm paraphrasing here, Frankie deserves better than a studio with no natural light."

"Okay, that's enough," Beckett says, face completely red now.

"I'm just saying," Richard grins, clearly enjoying himself, "I've watched you be in love with this woman for years while pretending you weren't. So forgive me if I'm a little smug about you two finally figuring it out."

I'm staring at Beckett, who looks like he wants to disappear. "The flowers were you?" I ask again.

He sighs. "Yeah."

"Every year?"

"Every year."

"You are such a sap," I say, but my smile is wide and full of love.

"Don't tell anyone," he mutters.

Richard laughs. "Oh, I'm telling everyone."

"Please don't," Beckett mutters, but there's no heat in it.

Richard heads toward the elevator, plate in hand, still chuckling. "Enjoy the rest of your day, you two."

The doors close behind him.

I turn to Beckett slowly. "Ugh, I love that man"

"He's a menace," Beckett says, but he's smiling. "I'm sorry about all that."

"Don't be." I lean across the counter and kiss him. Quick but sweet. "The flowers were a nice touch."

"You're never going to let me live that down, are you?"

119

"Not even a little bit."

He shakes his head, pulling me closer. "What are you doing this afternoon?"

My phone buzzes on the counter. I glance at it.

TALIA

> Coffee? I know I saw you this morning but I want actual catch up time. Without interruptions.

I show Beckett the text.

"Go," he says before I can ask.

"You sure?"

"Frankie." He cups my face. "Go see your friend. I'll be here when you get back."

"You better be."

"Promise."

I kiss him once more, then head to the bedroom to change. I'm still wearing his hoodie and sleep shorts—not exactly coffee date appropriate.

Twenty minutes later, I'm showered and dressed in jeans, a vintage band tee, and my favorite leather jacket. I grab my bag and keys.

"I'm heading out," I call.

Beckett appears in the doorway, takes one look at me, and smiles. "You look good."

"I know." I grin. "Don't do something stupid while I'm gone."

"No promises."

I flip him off as I walk out. He's laughing.

Talia's already at the café when I arrive, sitting at a corner table with two iced teas waiting.

"Hey," I say, sliding into the seat across from her.

"Hey yourself." She looks me over, smiling. "You look good."

"Yeah?"

"Yeah. Relaxed. Happy." She tilts her head. "So I'm guessing you two *really* worked it out after I left?"

My face heats. "We talked. And... other things."

"Other things?" She grins. "Do I want to know?"

"Probably not."

She laughs, taking a sip of her tea. "I'm glad, Frankie. Really."

"Me too." I fidget with my straw. "I'm sorry you had to come back early. You were supposed to be in Tuscany."

"Don't apologize. We wanted to be here." Her expression softens. "You're family. That's more important than a vacation."

"Still. I feel bad. You literally just got married."

"And we'll go back." She waves it off. "Tuscany will still be there. You needed us."

"How was it though? Before I ruined it?"

"You didn't ruin anything." But she's smiling now, eyes going a little dreamy. "It was perfect, honestly. We stayed at this villa in the hills. Stone walls, vineyard views, the whole thing."

"Very romantic."

"Extremely. Stellan pretended to be unimpressed but I caught him staring at the sunset like it personally moved him."

I laugh. "That sounds like him."

"We spent most days just... existing. No schedule. No plans. Just wine and food and each other." She sighs contentedly. "It was exactly what we needed."

"I'm glad." I mean it. "You guys deserve that."

"So do you," she says pointedly.

"Yeah, well. We're working on it."

"Good." She leans forward. "Now tell me everything. How bad was the groveling?"

I open my mouth to answer when the door chimes.

It wouldn't have mattered except Talia's expression changes. Her eyes go alert. Her spine stiffens immediately.

I turn.

Lorraine and Lexi Collette walk in. It's like they're stalking me. They would never come to this place otherwise.

Perfect. Fucking perfect.

"You've got to be kidding me," I mutter.

Talia's hand finds mine across the table. "Want to leave?"

"No." I sit up straighter. "I'm not running from them."

Lorraine spots us first. Her eyes narrow. She leans over to Lexi, whispering something—no doubt telling her I'm here.

Lexi's head whips around. When she sees me, her face twists into something ugly. They start stomping toward us.

"Here we go," I say under my breath.

Lexi reaches our table first, Lorraine a step behind like always.

"Well, well," Lexi says, voice dripping fake sweetness. "If it isn't the trashy bartender and the mail order bride. What a pair you make."

I don't flinch. "Lexi."

Talia goes very still beside me. "What did you just say?" Her voice quivering.

"Oh, you heard me." Lexi tilts her head. "Everyone knows what the Shadow Brides really are. A shopping service for men who can't find wives the normal way. Tell me, did Stellan pick you out of a catalog?"

The café goes quiet around us. Talia's hand releases mine. She stands slowly.

"Shouldn't you be in jail?" Talia asks, voice like ice.

Lexi's smile sharpens. "Bail, darling. It's a wonderful thing when you have money of your own."

"Right." Talia's voice doesn't waver. "Because assaulting someone is totally defensible when mommy dearest can write a check."

Lexi's smile falters slightly.

Talia tilts her head. "You know, I always wondered why you were so bitter about the program."

Lexi blinks. "Excuse me?"

"You applied," Talia says smoothly.

Lexi stiffens. "That's a lie."

"It's documented." Talia's voice doesn't lift. "You thought being blonde and adjacent to power made you eligible."

Lexi's mouth opens, but nothing comes out.

"Unfortunately," Talia continues, "they were looking for *actual* qualifications. Not headlines."

Color rises in Lexi's cheeks.

"Don't worry," Talia adds with a razor edged smile. "Rejection builds character. Maybe try that next."

"You both think status matters more than substance." I cross my arms. "You walk around like your last names give you power. But all you've got is your husbands' money and desperation."

"Excuse me?" Lexi's voice rises.

"You heard me." I step closer. "You're desperate. You threw a glass at my face because I have what you want. Not the name or the money—you've got plenty of that. You want someone to actually choose you."

Lexi's face goes red. "Beckett chose me—"

"Three dates ten years ago doesn't count as being chosen," Talia cuts in smoothly, rolling her eyes. "That's barely a trial period."

"We had a connection—"

"You had proximity," I correct. "That's all you've ever had."

Lorraine steps forward, trying to regain control. "You girls are adorable. Truly. But let's not pretend either of you belong in our world."

"Your world?" Talia laughs. It's not a nice sound. "You mean the world where you've burned through three husbands for their bank accounts? Where everyone knows you groomed your daughter to do the same?"

Lorraine's composure cracks. "How dare you—"

"Oh, I dare." Talia's smile is sharp. "Because unlike you, I don't have to manipulate men into loving me. Stellan chose me. Not my connections. Not my pedigree. Me."

"He bought you—"

"He found me," Talia corrects. "He paid a service to find me, when your mother was right there begging anyone of worth to look at her twice."

Lexi's hands clench into fists. "You think you're so special—"

"I don't think," Talia says calmly. "I know. Because when Stellan looks at me, he sees a partner. Not a trophy. Not a transaction. And that terrifies you because you've never had that."

"And you," I turn to Lexi. "You came into my bar, assaulted me, and expected Beckett to what? Feel sorry for you? Finally see you?"

"He would have if you hadn't—"

"If I hadn't what? Existed?" I laugh. "Beckett didn't want you before I came along. He definitely doesn't want you now. You were a mistake he made once and learned from."

Lexi's breathing hard now. "You don't deserve him."

"Maybe not." I shrug. "But he married me anyway. Not you. Me. And no amount of bail money or fake tears is going to change that."

"You think this is over?" Lexi's voice shakes with rage.

"I think you lost years ago," I say simply. "You just haven't accepted it yet."

They turn to leave. But Lexi stops, looks back, pulling out her phone.

"What are you doing?" I ask.

She doesn't answer. Just holds it up, filming us.

"Lexi," Lorraine warns.

"No." Lexi's smile is vicious now. "I want everyone to see this."

She starts talking to the camera, voice shifting into something sweet and broken.

"Hi everyone. I'm here at a café where I just ran into Francine DeLuca—sorry, Francine *Harrington* now." Her voice cracks perfectly. "The woman who violently attacked me at The Well at the Onyx Hotel yesterday when I tried to confront her about what she did to my fiancé, Beckett Harrington. Yes, my fiancé. The man I've loved for years. The man she sexually assaulted."

My blood runs cold.

"That's right," Lexi continues, tears falling now. "She got him so drunk he could barely walk. He couldn't speak clearly. Couldn't think straight. He was incapacitated. And she dragged him to a Vegas chapel and forced him to marry her. He couldn't consent—not to the marriage, not to anything that happened that night. And she *knew* that. She planned it. She targeted a powerful man, got him intoxicated, and assaulted him. That's what this is. Sexual assault. Coercion. Entrapment."

"Stop—" I start.

"She's threatening me again," Lexi sobs. "Because I'm the only one brave enough to say it. Beckett Harrington is a victim. He was raped. She raped him. And now she's parading around with his ring on her finger like she didn't destroy his life. Like she didn't violate him in the worst possible way."

Talia grabs my arm. "Don't react. That's what she wants."

"Her friend knows," Lexi says to the camera. "Talia Rothwell—another woman who manipulates wealthy men for money. They're both predators. And they're standing right here, threatening me for telling the truth. Look at her face. She knows what she did. She knows she assaulted him and she doesn't even care."

I can't breathe.

"If this was a man doing this to a woman, he'd be in prison," Lexi says, voice trembling with carefully measured outrage. "But she's a woman, and he's rich and powerful, so no one's protecting him." She swallows hard, eyes a little too wide. "I went to that bar to confront her. I told her I knew what she did. And she threw a glass at my face."

Her voice tightens, but she pushes through.

"I ducked. The glass hit the wall and exploded—and suddenly she's the one bleeding? Somehow, I'm the monster?" She shakes her head. "I was in shock. I even tried to help her. And she shoved me. That's what she does. She lashes out. She hurts people who get in her way—and then turns herself into the victim."

She's sobbing now. Full performance.

"Beckett, if you're watching this—I love you. I'm fighting for you. And I won't stop until you're free from her. Until everyone knows what she really is. A rapist. A predator. Someone who belongs in prison, not in your bed."

She ends the video. Looks at me with pure hatred.

"Let's see how your husband explains that," she says sweetly.

She posts it. Right there. I watch her thumb move.

Within seconds, her phone starts buzzing. Notifications flooding in.

"Good luck with your life," Lexi says, flicking her hair over her shoulder. "What's left of it."

They walk out with Talia and I standing there. Frozen.

That one word keeps echoing in my head.

Rapist.

CHAPTER 14

Beckett

FRANKIE LEFT AN HOUR AGO TO MEET TALIA FOR coffee. She was smiling when she kissed me goodbye, said something about catching up properly.

I watched her leave feeling lighter than I have in days. We're good. *Finally* good.

I head to Stellan's office because Cal texted saying he was there and I should stop by. I should talk to him anyway, both of them really.

Cal's already there when I arrive, sprawled in one of the leather chairs like this is his house not a corporate office.

"Well, well," Cal says, grinning. "The newlywed graces us with his presence."

"Still not funny," I mutter, dropping into the chair across from him.

Stellan looks up from his laptop, smirking. "Talia just texted. Said she's with Frankie."

"Yeah, they're catching up."

"And you two are...?" One brow arches, smug as hell. He knows exactly what we are—he just wants to see if I'lll say it out loud.

"We're good," I say, and I mean it. "Really good."

Cal smirks. "So the groveling worked?"

"It wasn't groveling—"

"It was absolutely groveling."

My phone starts buzzing. Then buzzing again. And again.

I pull it out. Notifications are flooding in. Dozens. Hundreds.

"What the hell?" I unlock the screen.

Cal sits up. "What's wrong?"

I don't answer, I can't. Because I'm staring at a video that already has fifty thousand views.

Lexi's face fills the screen. Tears streaming. Voice breaking.

I turn up the volume without thinking.

"Hi everyone. I'm here at a café where I just ran into Francine DeLuca—sorry, Francine Harrington now." Her voice cracks, too perfect to be real.

My spine goes rigid.

Stellan stands beside me, unmoving. Cal swears low under his breath. But I can't tear my eyes away from the screen.

"The woman who violently attacked me at The Well at the Onyx Hotel yesterday when I tried to confront her about what she did to my fiancé, Beckett Harrington. Yes, my fiancé. The man I've loved for years. The man she sexually assaulted."

The words shock my entire system, almost stopping my heart.

"That's right," Lexi goes on, tear tracks visible, perfectly lit. "She got him so drunk he could barely walk. He couldn't speak clearly. Couldn't think straight. He was incapacitated. And she dragged him to a Vegas chapel and forced him to marry her."

I can't move.

"She planned it. She targeted a powerful man, got him intoxicated, and assaulted him. That's what this is. Sexual assault. Coercion. Entrapment."

"Stop—" Frankie's voice—distorted in the video—cuts in. I know that tone. Shock. Fury. Pain.

Lexi presses harder.

"She's threatening me again, because I'm the only one brave enough to say it. Beckett Harrington is a victim. He was raped. She raped him."

The word makes my stomach turn.

"She's parading around with his ring on her finger like she didn't destroy his life. Like she didn't violate him in the worst possible way."

I clench my fists at my sides.

"Talia Rothwell—another woman who manipulates wealthy men for money. They're both predators. And they're standing right here, threatening me for telling the truth. Look at her face. She knows what she did."

Stellan doesn't look away from the screen. "We should've muzzled her after she was arrested."

"If this was a man doing this to a woman, he'd be in prison," Lexi says. Her voice trembles like it's been coached. "But she's a woman, and he's rich and powerful, so no one's protecting him. I went to that bar to confront her. I told her I knew what she did. And she threw a glass at my face."

She swallows. Her gaze flicks up like she's searching for sympathy in an audience that isn't there.

"I ducked. The glass hit the wall and exploded—and suddenly she's the one bleeding? Somehow, I'm the monster?" She pauses for long enough to wipe a fake tear from her eye. "I was in shock. I even tried to help her. And she shoved me. That's what she does. She lashes out. She

131

hurts people who get in her way—and then turns herself into the victim."

She's sobbing now. The mascara is probably waterproof, but she timed the cracks in her voice just right.

"Beckett, if you're watching this—I love you. I'm fighting for you. And I won't stop until you're free from her. Until everyone knows what she really is. A rapist. A predator. Someone who belongs in prison, not in your bed."

The video ends.

Cal grabs my phone and starts scrolling. His expression darkens the more his thumb moves.

"It's everywhere," he says. "On all of the social media platforms. Already trending."

I can't speak.

Stellan's watching me. "Beckett—"

"She called Frankie a rapist." My voice doesn't sound like mine.

"I know."

"She said I couldn't consent."

"I know."

"That's a fucking lie." My hands are shaking. "I was sober. I remember everything. Every second of that night."

"I believe you," Stellan says calmly. "But look at the comments."

Cal hands me the phone back.

I scroll.

@vegasnightlife: *Oh my god is this real??*

@harringtonfan2024: *Poor Beckett. He deserves so much better.*

@stripgossip: *She got him DRUNK and MARRIED him?? That's literally assault*

@justiceforgirls: *This woman is dangerous*

The rage bursts through my veins. White hot and all consuming. I stand so fast my chair tips backward.

"I'm going to destroy her."

Stellan doesn't blink. "Good. Let's make a plan."

He's already moving, pulling his laptop around, fingers flying across the keys. This is what he does. Crisis management. Reputation control. He's done this a thousand times for a thousand different clients.

But this time it's personal.

"First," Stellan says, voice calm and clinical, "we need to contain the damage. The video's viral, but we can control the narrative from here."

"How?" I'm still shaking. "It's everywhere. Everyone has already seen it and formed their own opinions."

"Because we move faster and smarter." He pulls up his phone, already texting. "I'm calling our legal team. Defamation. False accusations. We hit her with everything."

Cal's watching the video again, scrolling through comments. "It's trending. #JusticeForLexi. #ProtectBeckett."

"That changes in the next hour," Stellan says. "We release a statement. From you. Directly refuting every claim she made."

"A statement won't—"

"It will if we do it right." Stellan looks at me. "You were sober. You remember the night. We get ahead of this before it spirals further."

"And Frankie?" My voice cracks and my chest tightens. "I need to go to her."

"Not yet." Stellan's voice is firm. "We handle this first. You go to her with a plan, not just panic."

Cal stands. "What do you need from me?"

"Contact your network. Anyone with media pull. We need

counter narratives out within the hour. Friends, colleagues, anyone who knows Frankie or Beckett. Get them talking."

"On it." Cal's already dialing.

Stellan turns back to me. "Sit. We're drafting your statement now. I will call Richard. He'll want to know before this hits his desk."

"He probably already knows."

"Then we make sure he knows we're handling it." Stellan pulls up a blank document. "Start talking. Tell me exactly what happened that night. Every detail. We need the truth on record."

I take a breath. Force myself to focus.

"I was sober. Completely. I'd been nursing the same beer all night because I wanted to remember everything. Frankie was drunk—happy drunk. She pulled me onto the Strip, found a chapel, and asked me to marry her."

"Did you hesitate?"

"No."

"Did she force you?"

"Of course not." I scoff, if anything I was the one who took advantage of the situation.

"Did you sign the marriage license willingly?"

"Yes. I wanted to marry her. I've wanted to marry her for years."

Stellan types as I talk, his fingers never slowing.

"Good. That's what we lead with. Your consent. Your choice. Your clarity." He glances up. "Now we add the facts. Lexi was never your fiancée. You went on three dates six years ago. No ring. No proposal. No relationship."

"She's delusional."

"She's calculated," Stellan corrects. "This isn't delusion. This is strategy. She's trying to destroy Frankie's reputation.

She's pissed that you got married and she wasn't your choice. Her ego is damaged. But she's smart."

Cal comes back, phone still in hand. "I've got five people ready to post. What's the message?"

"Beckett Harrington is happily married to Frankie. Any claims to the contrary are false and defamatory. Lexi Collette is facing criminal charges for assault. Full stop."

"Got it."

My phone buzzes again. A text from Frankie.

FRANKIE

Did you see it?

My hands shake as I type back.

Yes. I'm with Stellan. We're handling it. Are you okay?

Three dots appear. My heart soars before they disappear. Only to appear again a moment later.

FRANKIE

No.

My heart shatters.

"Stellan—"

"We need to move fast," he says, already pulling up documents. "This is damage control now."

I can't focus. Can't think past the word *rapist* echoing in my head.

Lexi called Frankie a rapist.

On camera. To thousands of people. Tens of thousands now.

My wife. The woman I love. The woman I *chose* to marry.

And Lexi's painting her as a predator.

Stellan's phone rings. He glances at the screen. "It's Talia."

He answers, putting it on speaker. "Talk to me."

"We're coming to your office." Talia's voice is tight. Controlled. "Is Beckett there?"

"I'm here," I say immediately. My voice sounds strangled.

"Good. We'll be there in ten minutes."

"How is she?" I ask, and I'm not sure I want the answer.

A pause. "Not good, Beckett. She's... she's trying to hold it together, but this is bad."

My chest constricts. I can barely breathe.

"We're leaving now. Just—be ready."

The line goes dead.

Ten minutes. Frankie will be here in ten minutes and I need to have my shit together.

But all I can see is that video. Lexi's tears. Her lies. The comments already believing her.

Rapist.

Predator.

Dangerous.

I force myself to focus. Stellan's already typing, pulling up documents, making calls.

My hands won't stop shaking.

Stellan's phone rings again. He glances at the screen, frowns, and answers on speaker.

"It's getting worse." The voice belongs to one of Stellan's PR team. "Dr. Carl Hallingsworth just posted a video. It's already got twenty thousand views."

My blood turns to ice. "What?"

"He's corroborating Lexi's story. Says he was engaged to Frankie, that she has a pattern of manipulating wealthy men, that she's unstable and dangerous."

"Pull it up," Stellan snaps.

Cal's already on it, finding the video on his phone. He hits play.

Carl's face appears. White coat visible in the background like he planned it.

"I normally wouldn't speak publicly about private matters," Carl starts, voice measured and sympathetic. "But after seeing Lexi Collette's video, I feel morally obligated to come forward."

"That son of a bitch," I growl.

"Francine DeLuca and I were together for nearly seven years. Our families had an arrangement—one that both she and I honored and built a life around. We were planning our future together. But then she met Beckett Harrington, and everything changed."

My stomach drops.

"She became distant. Started picking fights. And then, seemingly overnight, she was married to him in Vegas. She didn't even have the decency to end things with me first. She just... moved on. Left me devastated."

"That's not—" I start.

"Keep watching," Stellan says grimly.

Carl's expression melts into something much darker. "But it gets worse. When I tried to reach out to understand what happened, she retaliated. She went to my hospital administration with false claims that I had physically assaulted her during our relationship. Complete fabrications. Lies designed to destroy my career and my reputation."

"What?" Cal straightens.

"And she succeeded," Carl continues, voice breaking slightly. "I was fired. My medical license is under review. Everything I'd worked for was gone because of her vindictive lies. The damage is permanent. My reputation is tarnished. My career derailed. All because I loved the wrong woman."

He looks directly at the camera now. Trying his best to act like he is distraught about this whole thing.

"I'm speaking out because I see the same pattern repeating. She targeted Beckett. Got him intoxicated. Trapped him in a marriage he didn't consent to. And when he tries to get free? She'll destroy him too. Just like she destroyed me."

His voice drops. "If you know Frankie, please be careful. She's charming, manipulative, and dangerous. And if Beckett is watching this—get out now. Before it's too late. Before she ruins your life the way she ruined mine."

The video ends.

Cal sets his phone down slowly. "That's bad."

"That's the game," Stellan corrects. "He's positioning himself as the victim. The scorned lover. The man she broke. By doing that, he may be able to get his life back to what he believes that he deserves."

"He's a fucking liar." My fists clench. "They dated for maybe six months when she was nineteen. She ended it because he was controlling and her parents were forcing it. There was no seven year relationship. No assault claims. None of it."

"Doesn't matter." Stellan's already typing. "The internet doesn't fact check. They see a doctor in a white coat, hear him say she got him fired with false claims, and they believe it."

"So what do we do?"

"We finish him." Stellan stands, walking towards us. "Carl made a mistake. He went on record with lies. That's actionable. If he's claiming she filed false assault reports, we can pull hospital records. Prove he's lying."

"He was fired," I say. "I know that much. Because I'm the one who put the ball in motion."

Stellan looks up sharply. "What?"

"After the hospital. When Frankie got stitches. Carl was

harassing her. He wouldn't let her leave, he went so far that he put hands on her." My jaw clenches. "I called Dr. Kooper. Told him either Carl walked or the Harrington funding did. He was fired within the hour."

Cal whistles low. "So he's not lying about being fired. Just about why."

"Exactly." Stellan's already typing faster. "He's twisting the truth. Making himself the victim when he was the aggressor."

"So we have proof," I say.

"We have your word. We need documentation." Stellan picks up his phone. "I'm calling Kooper. Getting the official record of why Carl was terminated. If it's what you say, we can use it to destroy his credibility."

"Do it," I say.

"Then we find out why." Stellan's fingers fly across his keyboard. "Because if Carl was fired for harassment, and he's out here claiming it was false assault allegations, that's defamation. Against Frankie and against the hospital."

My phone buzzes. I glance down.

RICHARD

Five minutes out.

I look at the time. Frankie should be here any second.

Cal moves to the window, looking down at the street below. "Social media's still exploding. The videos are everywhere."

"How bad?" I ask, even though I don't want to know.

"Trending on three platforms. Hundreds of thousands of views combined. The comments are..." He turns to look at me, cutting off what he was about to say. "You don't want to read them."

My hands clench into fists.

Stellan's on the phone, all business now. "Dr. Kooper. Stellan Rothwell. I need the official termination documentation for Dr. Carl Hallingsworth. Yes, immediately. Email it to me in the next ten minutes."

He nods and hangs up. Clearly he got what he wanted. The small smile on his face gives that away.

"It's coming," he says. "Once we have that, we dismantle Carl's entire story."

"And Lexi?" I ask.

"Already working on it. Her assault charges are public record. We use that. Show she's the one with a history of violence, not Frankie."

The door opens.

I turn.

Frankie stands in the doorway. Talia's right behind her, hand on her shoulder like she's holding her up.

But it's Frankie's face that stops my heart.

She's pale. Eyes red and swollen like she's been crying the entire ride here. Her hands are shaking. She's still wearing my hoodie, arms wrapped tight around herself.

"Beckett," she whispers.

CHAPTER 15
Frankie

THE TEARS WON'T STOP.

I'm trying not to make any noise, trying not to sob or wail or rage the way that I want to. I'm just standing in the elevator while salty droplets fall down my cheeks, slipping to my lips.

Talia's hand is on my arm. "Frankie," she says. "Beckett loves you. You know that, right?"

I nod. She thinks that I agree with her. That I know. But he shouldn't love me. Not anymore. Not after this. He knows she was lying, but the fact that I'm bringing all of this to him, that's what should make him stop, make him turn away from me.

"We're going to fix this," Talia continues. "Stellan already has a plan. Beckett put out a statement. They're handling it."

Handling me. The crisis. The problem that needs solving.

The elevator dings and the doors slide open. my feet move without permission, they're shaky as they make their way down the hall to Stellan's office. Talia stays close to me, almost touching my arm, she's watching me like she thinks I might fall over onto the floor right here.

Beckett's in the office. I just have to make it there.

He knows the Harrington name is trending next to words like assault and predator because of me.

He should walk away. Cut his losses. Protect what's left of his family's reputation.

Talia squeezes my arm. "He's not going to leave you."

I stop.

"I know what you're thinking," she says. "And you're wrong."

"You don't know that." My voice cracks. These are the first words I've spoken since the café.

"I do."

"Talia, I'm a PR nightmare for his family. I've ruined—"

"*You* haven't ruined anything." That's easy for her to say. She's not the one dragging the Harrington name through hell.

"He should leave me." The truth feels metallic on my tongue. "Anyone would."

"Good thing Beckett's not most people."

I shake my head. She doesn't understand. This isn't about love anymore. This is survival. Legacy. Everything the Harringtons built over decades.

I'm the bomb that's about to blow that all to the ground.

We reach the door, finally. My hand is hovering over the knob. He's on the other side waiting for me, probably already firm in his decision. I'll see it in his eyes the second I walk in.

I open the door, though I'm not sure that I want to. Beckett's already turning. Like he knew I was there before the handle had even moved.

I take a deep breath—bracing for the anger, the regret I know I'll see—before i lock eyes with him.

But that's not what I'm met with. He looks terrified. Not at me, but *for* me.

The relief hits so hard my knees almost give out. He's not leaving. He's not done. He's just worried.

"Beckett," I whisper. That's when my knees fully give out.

He crosses the room before I can fall apart completely. His arms wrap around me, pulling me in tight. One hand goes to the back of my head, the other around my waist.

I collapse into him. The sobs I've been holding back since the café rip out of me.

"I've got you," he murmurs into my hair. "I've got you."

The door opens again behind us.

"Frankie."

Richard just walked in the room. Fucking great. I can't look at him. Can't face him. Not when his family name is being destroyed because of me.

Beckett's arms tighten, like he knows what's going through my mind he says, "It's okay. He's here to help."

I take my head out of Beckett's chest. Everyone around us is there to support us.

Stellan walks up to us and wordlessly hands me a piece of paper. Looking down, I see that it is a statement. A press release about this whole thing.

ROTHWELL STRATEGIC HOLDINGS *Official Statement on Behalf of the Harrington Family*

FOR IMMEDIATE RELEASE

Rothwell Strategic Holdings is issuing the following statement on behalf of Beckett Harrington and the Harrington family in response to false and defamatory claims circulating on social media.

Regarding the allegations made by Ms. Alexandra Collette:

The claims that Mr. Harrington was intoxicated or unable to consent on the evening of his marriage to Francine

Harrington are categorically false. Mr. Harrington was fully sober, aware, and entered into marriage willingly and enthusiastically. No coercion, manipulation, or intoxication occurred.

Ms. Collette's assertion that she was engaged to Mr. Harrington is demonstrably false. Mr. Harrington and Ms. Collette attended several social events together approximately six years ago. There was no romantic relationship, no engagement, and no commitment of any kind.

Regarding the allegations made by Dr. Carl Hallingsworth:

Dr. Hallingsworth's claims that he was terminated from St. Avelyn's Medical Center due to false assault allegations are provably untrue. Official hospital records, provided by Chief Administrator Dr. Kenneth Kooper, confirm that Dr. Hallingsworth was terminated for physically restraining Mrs. Francine Harrington and refusing to allow her to leave the hospital. No assault allegations were filed by Mrs. Harrington or any other party.

Dr. Hallingsworth's claim of a seven year relationship with Mrs. Harrington is false. The two dated briefly when Mrs. Harrington was nineteen years old, a relationship she terminated.

Supporting Evidence:

Official documentation from St. Avelyn's Medical Center confirms Dr. Hallingsworth's termination for cause. Multiple witnesses at the hospital can corroborate the incident that led to his dismissal.

The marriage license and chapel records from Las Vegas confirm Mr. and Mrs. Harrington's marriage. The officiant and witnesses have provided statements affirming both parties were willing participants.

Associates, colleagues, and friends of both Mr. and Mrs. Harrington have provided voluntary statements affirming the legitimacy of their relationship and marriage.

Ms. Alexandra Collette was arrested and charged with assault following an incident at the Onyx Hotel. Criminal proceedings are ongoing. Multiple witnesses and security footage corroborate the assault.

Legal Action:

The Harrington family, in partnership with Rothwell Strategic Holdings, will be pursuing all available legal remedies for defamation against Ms. Alexandra Collette, Dr. Carl Hallingsworth, and any other parties engaged in making false and damaging statements.

No further comment will be made at this time.

Contact: Rothwell Strategic Holdings Press Office at press@rothwellstrategicholdings.com

I finish reading, the paper trembling in my hands.

They did this. All of this. For me.

Hospital records. Witness statements. Security footage. Cal's entire network vouching for us. Stellan drafting every word like a weapon. Richard backing it with the Harrington name.

Beckett defending me to the entire world.

They are going to war for me. I've never experienced this kind of pain and love at the same time.

The sobs rip out of me. Gasping, choking, can't breathe through them.

"I've got you," he murmurs into my hair. "I've got you."

I can't stop. Can't catch my breath. The tears won't stop and I'm shaking so hard my teeth chatter.

"Breathe, Frankie," he says quietly. "Just breathe."

I try. I can't. I gasp for any air I can get into my lungs.

"With me," he says calmly. "In. Out. Come on."

I force air into my lungs. It hurts.

"Good. Again."

I breathe, him setting the pace. Slowly, the gasping eases.

But the tears don't stop.

Richard looks at Stellan. "What's next? Legally."

"We file defamation suits against both Collette and Hallingsworth by end of business today," Stellan says. "Civil and criminal where applicable. We're also pursuing charges against Lorraine Collette for conspiracy."

"Timeline?"

"Months. Maybe a year for full resolution." Stellan doesn't sugarcoat it. "But the statement buys us immediate relief. Shifts the narrative."

Richard nods. "And the media plan?"

Cal speaks up. "My contacts are already pushing the counter narrative. By tonight, every major outlet will have the real story. We're also flooding social media with the truth— witness accounts, the hospital records, security footage from the Onyx."

"Spare no expense," he says quietly. Gently. But there's steel underneath. "I don't care what it costs. You protect my daughter."

My daughter.

He called me his daughter. I don't think. I just move.

I cross the room and throw my arms around Richard. His arms come around me immediately. Fatherly safety incases my heart in a veil of love.

"We've got you, sweetheart," he murmurs. "All of us."

I nod against his shoulder, unable to speak quite yet.

I take a breath and look at Stellan. "What else?" I finally start to feel everyone fall into place. There is a plan in place and everything is handled.

My phone buzzes in my pocket. Without thinking, I take it out and open up the message from the unknown number.

UNKNOWN NUMBER

> We know everything, rapist. 322 Onyx Residences Unit 2B. Penthouse now, right? The Dutch Wall where you work. We'll find you. You're going to pay for what you did to Beckett, Lexi, and Carl. We'll make you feel every second of it. You'll beg us to stop. We won't. You'll wish you were dead long before we finish.

The shock on my face is there before I can stop it. My eyes fly wide and I throw one of my hands to cover my mouth while I stare at the hate filled message.

Talia's there in a second, taking the phone from my shaking hands. Her face goes white, similar to the look I'm wearing, I'm sure.

"What?" Beckett's voice drops menacingly low. "What does it say?"

Talia's jaw clenches. Then she reads it out loud.

The room goes deadly silent.

"You're taking immediate leave from The Dutch Wall," Beckett says. "Effective right now."

"No—" I start.

"Frankie." Richard cuts in gentle but firm. "This isn't negotiable."

"I can't just—"

"You can and you will," Stellan says. "They know where you work. They're threatening your life. You're not going back until this is contained."

"Lena and Roxy can handle it," Cal adds. "You know they can."

I look around the room. Every single person is staring at me with the same expression.

This isn't a discussion. It's already decided.

"Okay, but just until this is settled. And I can do office work from a laptop in the apartment. My voice is regaining some of its strength. I can do this, we have a plan now.

Talia's still holding my phone. She looks at Stellan. "We need to bring in Opal. Now."

"Absolutely not." The words are out of my mouth before I can stop them.

Everyone turns to look at me.

"No," I say again, louder this time. "Not her. After what she did to you? To Stellan? No."

"Frankie—" Talia starts.

"She betrayed Stellan. She nearly destroyed everything. And you want to bring her in now?" I shake my head. "No way."

"She's the best at this," Stellan says quietly, reluctantly.

"I don't care—"

"Frankie." Talia's voice is calm. "I know what she did. We all do. But right now, we need someone who can find these threats and give us all the information that we need. She's the only one who can do it fast enough."

"There has to be someone else—"

"There isn't," Stellan says. "Not with her skill set. Not with her speed. Talia needs her help if we're going to get this taken care of right away."

I look at him. "You're okay with this?"

"No," he admits. "But I'm less okay with you being in danger."

Beckett's hand finds mine, he levels me with a look so filled with love and admiration that I can't say no. "We don't have a choice."

I hate this. I hate all of it.

"Fine," I whisper. "But I don't have to like it."

"You don't have to," Talia says. She's already typing. "But she'll help."

She hits send.

Less than ten seconds later, her phone buzzes.

She reads it, then looks up. "She's on it. Said she'll trace the number too."

My phone buzzes in Talia's hand. Continues to buzz again and again.

She looks at the screen. Her face goes pale. "Frankie—"

The TV on Stellan's wall flickers to life. Someone must have turned it on. A news anchor's face fills the screen, the chyron scrolling beneath her.

Viral Video Accuses Vegas Bartender of Sexual Assault

My stomach drops.

"Turn it up," Richard says hoarsely.

Cal grabs the remote. The anchor's voice fills the room.

"—story has exploded across social media in the past few hours. Alexandra Collette posted this emotional video earlier today, claiming that Francine Harrington, manager of the high-end Dutch Wall bar at the Onyx Hotel, sexually assaulted billionaire heir Beckett Harrington—"

"Turn it off," Beckett says.

"Wait." Stellan's eyes are locked on the screen.

The anchor continues. "We're now receiving reports that multiple people have come forward with similar allegations against Mrs. Harrington, claiming a pattern of predatory behavior—"

"What?" I choke out.

My phone won't stop buzzing. Talia's holding it like it might explode.

The news cuts to a new face. A woman I've never seen before, crying into the camera.

"She did the same thing to my brother," the stranger sobs. "Got him drunk. Forced herself on him. Ruined his life—"

"That's not real," I whisper. "I don't even know her—"

But nobody's listening to me. They're all staring at the screen. The lie that the Collette's spreading in real time.

At my life crumbling before our very eyes.

CHAPTER 16
Beckett

I haven't slept in three days.

I push open the door to Stellan's office and stop.

The place looks like a war room.

Laptops cover every surface. Whiteboards line the walls, filled with timelines, phone numbers, and social media handles. Empty coffee cups stack on the conference table. Papers are everywhere—printed threats, legal briefs, media strategy docs.

The divider's open. The entire massive space spreads out before me—what used to be two separate offices before Stellan insisted on combining them. He wanted one office so he could always be near Talia. She needed her own space, room to think without him hovering. They bickered about it for weeks until Talia proposed the divider as a compromise. Stellan agreed, probably because he knew he'd won the bigger battle—keeping her close.

Right now, the divider's wide open. No privacy when it's all hands on deck.

Stellan's at his desk, phone pressed to his ear. He sees me and holds up one finger.

I drop into the chair across from him. Every muscle in my body aches.

He hangs up, and turns his attention to me. "You look like hell."

"I feel worse." I blow out a breath and scrub my hands down my face.

"How is she?" Talia asks from across the room.

"Not good." I just came from the penthouse. Before I left, I made her promise me that she wouldn't leave. "She wants to fight for herself. She wants to get shit done along with us. I just can't risk her getting hurt."

My father shifts in his chair. "Maybe one of us should go back."

"She needs space right now," I say. "I know Frankie. Being crowded when she's like this would only make it worse."

Talia nods. "She'll come out when she's ready."

"Still getting threats?" Stellan asks.

"Her phone won't stop. We've changed her number twice. But it doesn't seem to matter, they keep finding her, almost immediately." My hands curl into fists. "Death threats. Rape threats. People saying they know where she is, what they're going to do to her."

Stellan's jaw tightens. "Opal's tracing them."

"Not fast enough."

"I know."

Cal leans against the wall, arms crossed. "They're outside the Dutch Wall again. Signs, chants, the whole deal. Demanding the hotel cut ties with her. Health inspectors showed up this morning—'anonymous tip.'"

"Let me guess," I say. "They found violations."

"Nothing legitimate. But it doesn't matter. The optics are bad."

I lean back. Every part of me aches. "We put out the statement. We had witnesses. Hospital records. Everything."

"And?" My father asks.

"Lexi posted another video this morning."

Of course she did. What the hell is wrong with this girl?

Stellan pulls up his laptop, turns it toward me. "Two million views. She's crying, saying we're silencing victims. And that you're being brainwashed. That the Rothwells are weaponizing their wealth to destroy her."

I stare at Lexi's face on the screen. The tears. The performance.

"She's building a following," Stellan continues. "People are donating money for 'legal fees'. Calling her brave."

"And Carl?"

"Posting daily. Medical ethics. Corrupt powerful families. How doctors who protect women get destroyed." Stellan closes the laptop. "Half the internet thinks he's a hero."

A noise by the door stops everyone in the room dead.

I look up to see a woman standing in the doorway. She steps into the room, and for a second—just one—I don't recognize her.

Opal Greer.

But not the one we remember. Not the version that was blacklisted.

Her dark hair's longer now—hitting her elbow. It's almost pitch black and styled perfectly. Her hazel eyes are more green, brighter than before.

Gone are the blouses and fitted blazers, the skirts that hit just below the knee, the polite, invisible silhouette that made her easy to ignore.

She's in a dress—tight, sleek, blood dark. Burgundy, I think. Nothing flowy or loose. It fits her like a glove. Sky high heels and tights. Pitch black like her leather jacket. She doesn't look like she's here to be forgiven.

There's a folder in one hand, a slim black case in the other. Her grip is tight—white knuckled—but her posture is solid. Back straight. Shoulders square. She walks in like she knows every person in the room wants her gone and she doesn't give a shit.

She doesn't speak. Doesn't look around. Just crosses the floor, lays the file on the table in front of Stellan, and steps back.

She used to look like she worked for someone important.

Now she looks like she *is* someone important—and we just never got the memo.

You could've emailed this," Stellan says, voice like glass—cool, smooth, and meant to cut.

Opal doesn't blink. "I could have. But you needed to hear this in person. This isn't something you treat like a normal correspondence."

He leans back, impassive. "You shouldn't be here. You tried to destroy me. All in the name of revenge."

"What do you call blacklisting me?" she fires back. "All in the name of revenge, right? Look—do you want this or not? I didn't do it for you. I did it for Frankie. And Talia. Besides—" a small shrug, lips curved like a dare, "The Shadow Brides called. I'm getting married."

"Send him my condolences," Stellan says.

She smiles, burgundy lips smirking at us. "I don't think Dante will take them. He'll get a kick out of that."

From the back, Cal mutters, "You're nothing but a damaged girl."

Opal turns his way, lips splitting into a bigger smile. "One man's damaged goods is another man's prized possession."

She opens the folder. Laying it right in front of Stellan as he sits in his chair.

"Carl and Alexandra. Not allies—lovers. For at least three years now. I've got travel records, shared burner logs, ghost accounts, timestamps. Every leak, every post, every spin—coordinated."

Talia steps closer. Opal doesn't pause.

"Carl lost money when Frankie killed their deal. Alexandra lost Beckett. So they went after her. Together."

Opal flipped to the next page in the folder. "I tracked every fake post tied to Lexi's anonymous sources. They all ping back to the same server in Zurich. Paid for by a holding company that doesn't exist—except it does. Carl used it three years ago to bury an NDA violation."

Talia stepped in beside her, eyes scanning the documents as fast as Opal laid them down.

"The texts Frankie's been getting? The threats. They weren't random. They were timed. Dropped after key leaks. Designed to destabilize. To isolate her.

She flipped another sheet forward. "They created a pressure loop. Frankie gets attacked, the media reacts, Alexandra posts, Carl comments, and they spin it as victim blaming. Over and over, until public opinion turns just enough for their version to stick."

Stellan leaned back in his chair, expression unreadable. "So what do you want now? Redemption?"

Opal actually laughs. Like she genuinely couldn't believe he'd said it out loud.

"No," she says. "I already paid for it."

The words drop like stone into water. She doesn't look defensive. Her gaze meets Stellan's without so much as a blink.

"I said what needed to be said. Lost what there was to

159

lose. You just weren't looking when it happened."

Before I can stop myself, I reach for her arm. She pauses as my hand closes gently around her.

"Thank you," I say, and I mean it.

Opal looks at me. I can't read her. That is a bit scary. She gives a single nod. "Anytime."

"I can pay you."

A small smile tugs at her lips. The kind that says you're cute for trying. "This one's on me."

"What's your retainer now?"

That gets a real laugh. "You couldn't afford it."

She starts to turn, then stops, glancing back—only at Talia. "Folder. Top left. There's a card with a code." Her gaze doesn't waver. "Type the link manually. Use the etched passcode. Look into your camera—Talia's face is the key."

She turns fully this time, already walking.

"Two minute window. Don't waste it." She calls behind her as she walks away.

Her heels strike marble like clockwork, echoing behind her. She doesn't look back.

Talia moves, stepping toward the folder Opal left behind. She stops short, eyes narrowing at the upper corner.

"This isn't a firm's letterhead," she says, her voice tight.

She flips the last page. Hidden behind it—flush with the paper—is a matte black card. No branding. Just a thin line of rose gold text along the edge.

She reads what it says outloud. "TA 913 THRONE."

Printed faint beneath it, almost vanishing into the page is a link. rosebud-investigations.net/internal

She types it in. The screen flashes to enter the access code.

She keys it in. The next prompt appears, telling her to look here. The camera activates and Talia leans in.

One long chime. Two short tones.

All of a sudden, it unlocks to a pitch black screen. A crimson rose appears in the center that melts into black cherry around the edges. Underneath it says Rosebud Investigations.

"There isn't any other information here," she says. "Just where to contact and prices."

She clicks on it and it pops up.

Flat-rate engagement starting at $100,000 per case

Monthly retainer available for select clients— $75,000/month

"Well," Cal mutters, "guess getting blacklisted builds character."

Talia huffs a single breath—somewhere between a scoff and a laugh.

Stellan shakes his head once, dry. "Character. Is that what we're calling it now?"

Cal exhales a low laugh. "I don't care. I'm impressed."

Talia doesn't even glance at him. "That's because you're easily impressed."

His mouth pulls into a grin. "Still counts."

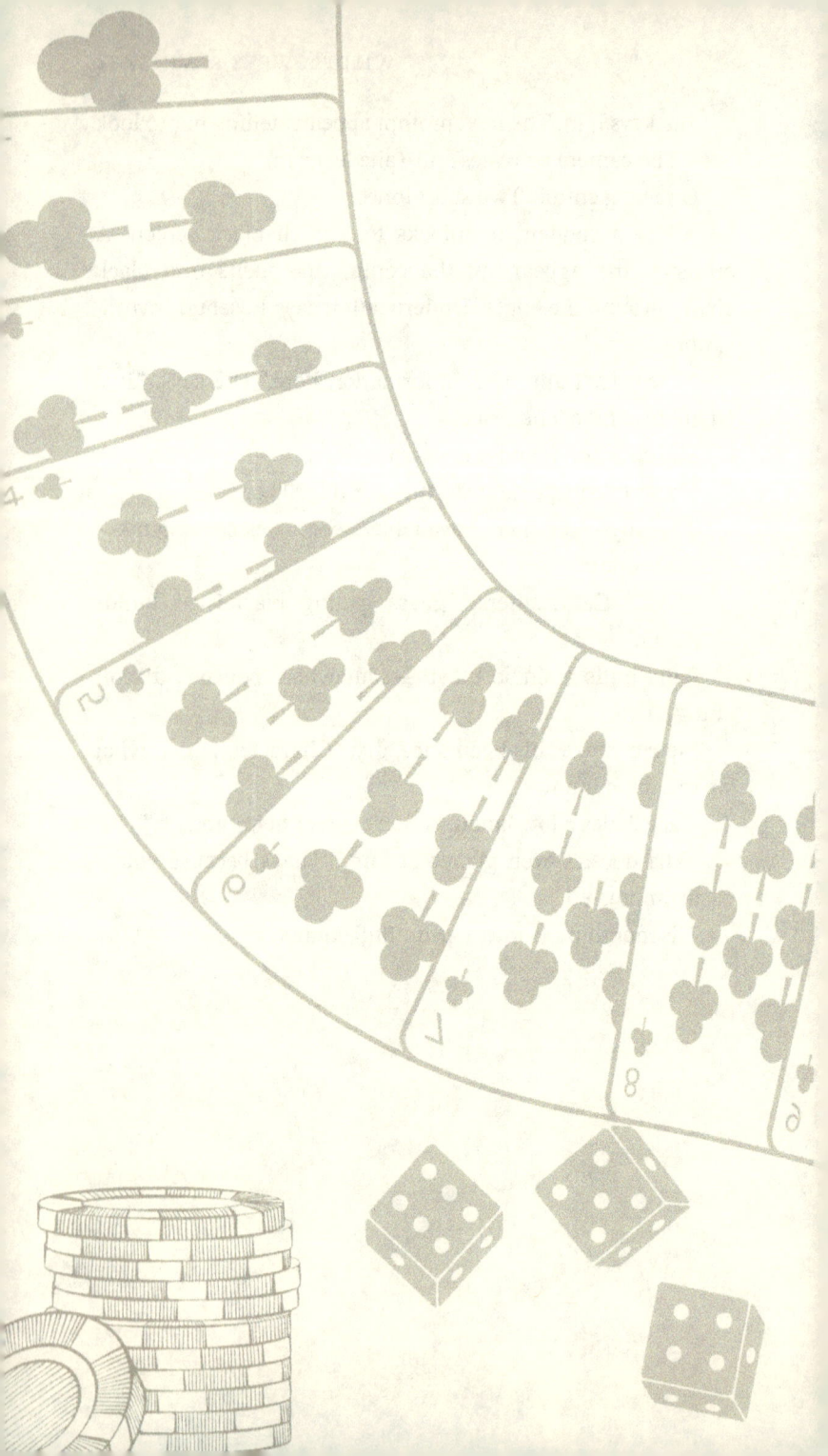

CHAPTER 17

Beckett

By the time I realize how long it's been since either of us moved, there's a knock.

The door opens, and Kate Loe steps in.

She's got two coffees in one hand, a white paper bag in the other, and that same calm, unshakable energy she carries into every room she walks into. Her bun's still perfect, blouse unwrinkled, even though I know she's been fielding calls since six and cancelling meetings Stellan never planned to take.

"Lunch," she says simply, setting the bag between Stellan and I.

I look at it, feel the hollow twist in my gut. I need this to be over. "I'm not hungry."

Kate doesn't push. Just places the coffee in front of me like she didn't hear it.

"Press is outside ONYX," she says. "Five cameras. Protesters are multiplying. There's a livestream crew from LA —it's already trending."

Stellan doesn't blink. "Let them wear themselves out."

Kate nods. "Security's in place. Back entrances locked

down. Statement draft's with legal—tone flagged, content's clean. You'll have it in ten."

"Scrub it again," he says.

"Already started." She turns to me next, hands over a folder. "Subpoena documents. Media counters are in the back."

"Kate," Stellan says.

Kate stops just short of the door.

"Clear my afternoon," Stellan says.

She nods. "It's already—"

The door swings open before she finishes.

Darlene DeLuca walks in. Her notebook's tucked under one arm. Warren follows. He doesn't speak. Just scans the room like he's assessing for structural weaknesses.

I don't move. But I feel Stellan freeze. His voice comes almost at a lethal level. "You have some goddamn nerve."

Darlene's eyes flick toward him—only briefly. Like looking longer would hurt more than she's willing to admit.

"We didn't come for you," she says.

"You're standing in *my* office," Stellan fires back.

Kate's already pulled her tablet to do whatever was next on her list—but she doesn't leave. She's not about to miss this.

Warren steps forward, hands loose at his sides. "We saw the videos."

Stellan doesn't blink. "You saw your daughter dragged through the mud and thought now was a good time to remember she exists?"

"Don't," Darlene warns, and for a second—just one— there's something behind her voice that sounds like grief. But it's buried deep.

"You disowned her." Stellan's voice is flat. "Don't try to pretend like it's anything different now."

Warren's jaw clenches. "We didn't come to fight."

"Then you shouldn't have come at all," Stellan says.

I stand. I don't remember deciding to.

"You came here for what, exactly?" I ask. "To say you saw the videos?"

Darlene meets my eyes. "Beckett—"

"She was alone," I cut in. "Alone when it mattered. You left, and she spent years pretending she didn't need you—because needing you hurt too much."

Warren's voice is low. "You think we didn't pay for that choice?"

"You think the pain counts if she didn't see it?" I step forward. "You don't get points for private guilt."

Talia adds her two cents to this whole thing. "You signed her over to Carl Hallingsworth. At eighteen. To a man twelve years older."

Warren doesn't flinch. But Darlene's fingers curl around the edge of her notebook like she's barely holding it together.

"We didn't sign the deal," she says.

My head snaps toward her. "What?"

"We didn't sign," Warren confirms, stepping closer. "The Hallingsworths planned it—yes. Carl was their prize. They bailed us out when we needed money. So they gave us an out. Arrange a marriage between Frankie and Carl. She was only seventeen and he was well into his late twenties."

"You refused?" The word tastes bitter. "Then why did everyone think—"

"Because Carl *wanted* them to," Darlene says.. "He leaked it. Told mutual clients it was already done. Said the papers were signed. All to box her in."

"Yet you never said anything to stop it," Stellan mutters.

Darlene nods. "By the time we realized what he was doing, the damage was public. No one questioned it—why would they? He was charming, successful. We were broke."

Warren's voice is like gravel. "The firm was bleeding out. My last contract tanked. We owed the Hallingsworth family more than we could cover. When we pushed back or even asked for more time, they had no problems telling us what we owed them."

"So you panicked and gave her up," I say.

"No." Darlene's eyes flash. "We *sold everything*. Liquidated what we had, took out private loans, and bought back our debt. Every Hallingsworth hand pulled out of our company before Frankie turned nineteen."

"You bought her freedom," Talia says softly.

"We thought we did," Warren replies. "But Carl didn't stop. He'd already poisoned the narrative."

"You could've told her," I say. Part of me understands how they're feeling. "You could've told her you didn't arrange her marriage."

Darlene's face cracks—just slightly. "We didn't think she'd believe us."

Warren glances away.

"She doesn't know," I say. "Not any of this."

"No," Darlene whispers. "She thinks we let it happen. Because we didn't stop the Hallingsworths fast enough. By the time we got wind, they were actually dating. Then they broke up. She wasn't speaking to us and neither were you."

Stellan stands slowly. His jaw is set, his hands relaxed at his sides.

"Carl's always gone for girls who haven't lived yet," Warren adds, disgust in every syllable. "The ones just old enough to sign contracts but not old enough to read between the lines."

"He's a fucking predator," I mutter.

Darlene nods. "He thought marrying her would make him legitimate."

"We refused," Warren says. "The Hallingsworths offered to forgive our debt if we signed. We said no. Took out the worst loan of our lives and bought them out—every share, every whisper of that agreement."

"It cost us everything," Darlene adds. "But we did it. For her."

My jaw is tight. I want to believe them. I *almost* do.

It would be easier not to. Easier to keep the anger on Frankie's behalf. That her own blood made her feel like an afterthought. Like she never mattered to begin with.

But when I look at Darlene now, I don't see indifference. I see a woman carrying guilt like a second spine. One that never healed right.

Warren hasn't taken his eyes off the floor since he explained how this whole situation cost them everything they held dear. That's not the look of a man defending his choices. That's someone who made the right one far too late.

Still, the part of me knows that Frankie had rough nights. I remember when she left home. She was lost and needed guidance. She needed them.

I've seen what power does to people in this city. I've watched men with money carve futures out of threats. Out of deals. This is Vegas afterall. The city with some of the biggest gambles.

I exhale, slow, feeling the air behind my ribs.

Frankie doesn't need people to protect her. She's done that herself for so damn long. But maybe—*maybe*—she deserves to know someone tried.

I turn away from the window, back toward the table, toward them.

"All right," I say quietly. "Let's fix it."

Warren lifts his head. Darlene blinks fast, like she's waiting for the catch.

"There is no forgiveness here," I add. "Not yet. Maybe not ever."

They nod. Accept it like they knew that was part of the deal.

The door slams open, hard enough to bounce against the wall.

Everyone turns.

Frankie fills the frame—barefoot on one side, the heel of her ruined shoe still gripped tight in her fist. Her dress clings to her in streaks of blood and grit. One shoulder's bare, the strap torn. Her hair's wet at the temple, matted with something darker than sweat. Her lip is split.

I stop breathing.

"Jesus—Frankie." The words rip out of me. I'm already moving, heart in my throat, to my wife who's covered in blood. "What the hell happened?"

She doesn't answer. Doesn't even look at me. Her eyes sweep the room.

"Baby," I say, voice cracking. "You're bleeding—your face —what—" My stomach turns. My fists curl. "Who the fuck let this happen?" I snap, spinning like I'll find someone to blame right now.

Frankie's still staring, still not speaking. But I see it in her eyes. She thinks this was us. That we called them. That we didn't protect her.

"What the fuck are they doing here?"

CHAPTER 18

Frankie

FUCK THIS.

I'm done playing dead.

I go to the closet and pull out a dress and some heels. I am tired of just staying here alone. Richard went to Stellan's. I'm guessing that's where everyone else went as well.

It's getting close to lunch. I might as well have it with them. I leave the penthouse without calling ahead. No heads up. No permission.

The car takes me to Rothwell Strategic.

No underground entrance. No tinted escape route. I step out at the main curb, in full daylight, dress blazing red under the Vegas sun.

I want to be seen.

I'm halfway to the doors when the first voice hits.

"Frankie DeLuca!"

It's shouted from across the sidewalk. I stop mid step and turn. There's a woman standing at the edge of the valet lane, face red, phone in one hand, coffee in the other. She's not alone, there's a group of them, six, maybe seven. All of them have their phones out and voices raised. They know who I am. They've been watching my life unravel.

The woman takes two steps forward before she hurls the coffee. before I don't have even a second to react.

It hits square across my chest—scalding, sticky, shocking. I gasp and stagger, hand flying up too late.

Someone else throws something—heavier. A can, maybe. It clips my shoulder and sends me sideways.

Then the shouting really starts.

"Fucking gold digger!"

"You think we don't know what you are?"

"Homewrecking bitch!"

They close in fast. Faces lit up with self righteous fury. Cameras aimed. I try to move, but a hand grabs my wrist. Another pushes from behind.

"Rapist!"

It cuts through everything. Louder than the crowd. Louder than my own heartbeat.

For a second, the world freezes.

Someone throws a phone. It bounces off my ribs. Another grabs at my dress, ripping the strap clean. I spin and elbow blindly, connect with something soft. Someone screams. Another shoves me into the pavement.

I hit hard—knees, palms, hips twisting in a weird direction. My vision blurs. There's blood now. Warm down my face. I taste it in my teeth.

They don't stop.

They want to break me open. Not just hurt me, but humiliate me until there's nothing left but the memory of what I used to be.

I see another hand cocking back with something heavy in it. A bag, maybe. A brick. I don't wait to find out.

I stand and run.

One heel snapped, dress torn, blood in my eyes—but I run.

Security finally floods out the doors—black suits, earpieces, and stun batons drawn all too late. I duck as two of them sprint past me, going for the crowd.

It doesn't matter.

I don't need rescuing.

I need to get inside.

I throw myself through the doors of Rothwell Strategic. Slamming into polished marble, I catch myself on bleeding palms. There's a scream somewhere behind me, a voice shouting. The lobby freezes.

The receptionist stops mid sentence, the interns in the elevator bank stop, one foot in the lift, the other on the marble tile of the lobby. There's a man with a clipboard that steps back like I'm something that will infect him.

I don't stop moving.

Blood's running down my cheek. I taste iron. My hands shake, but I jab the elevator button hard enough to split the skin again.

The doors slide open.

I step in alone.

Dress soaked. Face wrecked. Hair wild.

I hit the button for the executive floor and stare straight ahead as the doors seal shut—separating me from the noise, from the crowd, from the cameras.

I swear under my breath. When the doors open, I limp straight to Stellan's office and slam the door open.

I step in—barefoot on one side, the broken heel still gripped in my fist. Blood's drying down my neck, cracked in the lines of my palm. My dress is clinging to me in streaks of sweat, coffee, and grit. One strap's torn clean in two. My lip's split. My cheek's still bleeding.

They look at me like I've walked out of a war zone.

I clock every single face in the room.

Beckett. Stellan. Everyone there who I *thought* was my friend, people I *thought* I could trust.

They called my parents.

My heart's still racing. My vision's still edged with red. I taste metal and adrenaline and betrayal. I say it before I can stop myself.

"What the fuck are they doing here?"

Dad first. Always the fixer. Always the first hand out, the first apology halfway formed. Then my mom, slower, more careful, like I am just a little girl waiting to be put in timeout.

They saw the video.

They saw Carl.

They saw what the world thinks I am now.

"Frankie…" my dad starts. "Jesus. Your face—are you—"

Interesting. He looks like he's actually upset.

"Don't," I cut him off. My voice doesn't even sound like mine. It's raw. "Don't act surprised."

He flinches. My mom doesn't speak. Her eyes are glassy. Like she wants to pull me into her arms and knows she isn't allowed to anymore.

They're not looking at me like I'm their daughter. They're looking at me like I'm the headline. The girl in the dress. The girl in the blood. The one the internet named a monster.

"I didn't know," my mom whispers. "Carl—what he said, we didn't—" She cuts herself off. Because what is there to say?

My father starts to say something else, but it breaks the wrong nerve.

"Don't," I snap. "Don't you dare stand there like you get to worry now."

He blinks, stunned.

"I've been gone for *eight* years," I spit. "Eight. You disowned me and I started over—without you."

My mother's lip trembles. "Frankie—"

"No. You don't get to *Frankie* me. You did this."

Dad shakes his head. "That's not fair—"

"You sold me." The words come out before I can swallow them. "You sold me to save your business."

The room freezes.

"I found out from Opal," I say. "A few years ago. She showed me the contract. The clause with my name on it. You didn't just push me away—you traded me for the out. You gave them your only daughter and called it a merger."

Tears spill down my mother's face. "We never signed it."

Dad steps closer, voice breaking. "We didn't sell you, baby. We tried to protect you. We thought—God, we thought if we paid them back, they'd leave you alone."

I shake my head. I want to hate them. I really, really do. But looking at them now—my father's hand shaking, my mother trying not to touch me for fear I'll pull away—I see it.

All these years I thought that they wanted me to marry Carl or leave. I ran because I was scared they were going to disown me.

But looking at them now, maybe I overreacted. Maybe I was wrong all these years.

Mom finally reaches for me. Her hand hovers an inch from mine. "Please," she whispers. "Let us fix this."

I don't respond.

I don't have anything left to give them—not after today. Not after bleeding in the street while the world filmed it. Not after years of silence.

They're here now. They're sorry now. But now is too fucking late.

Still...the part of me that used to sit between them at

dinners, that used to believe in Sunday morning pancakes and business plans drawn on napkins, that part—it twitches.

They thought they could build something for me. Something that would make up for all of this.

"I can't think about that right now," I say, voice low. "Not after what just happened."

Dad nods slowly, like he expected it. "Okay," he says. "Okay."

Maybe—maybe—one day I'll be able to step forward again.

But not today.

"Come on," Beckett says softly in my ear. "Let's get you cleaned up."

I don't argue or look at my parents. I just follow.

My heel clicks unevenly on the tile. The other's still in my hand—gripped so tight my fingers ache. I don't let it go.

The door shuts behind us, and suddenly it's just quiet. White tile. Silver fixtures. A folded, pristine towel on the counter

Beckett grabs a first aid kit from under the sink and runs the water to get it warm.

I grab some supplies and stare down at my ruined outfit. "I've got it," I mutter.

"I know," he says, already crouching in front of me. "Still."

He doesn't touch me. Just looks up, waiting.

I sit.

The porcelain's cold through the torn dress. My palms sting when I set them down.

He starts with my knee. I watch the cloth turn red in his hands. He doesn't flinch.

"You should've called," he says under his breath.

"I didn't know it was coming."

He meets my eyes. "I think you did."

I look away. But I don't stop him.

His fingers trail up the back of my calf until they reach the edge of the torn dress. He hesitates.

I don't.

I shift just enough. An inch. Maybe less. But it's permission.

His hand slips higher.

My breath catches before I can swallow it.

He's still kneeling but now his hand is at the back of my thigh.

"You sure?" he asks.

God. His voice. It's low. Rough. Just for me.

I nod.

He stands slowly, rising between my knees until he's all I can see. His hands are sliding to my hips like he's memorizing their shape.

The towel slips from my lap. I don't care.

His thumb brushes just under the edge of the dress—bare skin, high on my thigh. His mouth finds my jaw. His lips linger. He kisses me like he's afraid I'll disappear again.

I don't feel weak anymore. I feel *worshipped*.

And when he dips his head lower, lips brushing the skin just above my heart, I whisper his name. "Beckett."

That's all it takes.

His mouth is on mine. One hand tangled in my hair, the other still gripping my hip.

I let him.

Because I love that he touches me like I'm everything.

When we walk back in, everyone's watching the screen.

No one's talking. No one even looks at me.

It's not shock this time. It's waiting. Something big is about to happen.

Stellan's leaning against the far table, arms crossed. The

screen behind him glows with a live news feed. Three headlines scroll beneath the anchor's voice.

Carl Hallingsworth under federal investigation. New evidence links Hallingsworth to cover ups, victim intimidation. Alexandra Collette deletes social accounts following public outcry.

Beckett stays close. I'm coiled so tight. I feel Beckett's arms wrap around me.

Talia turns toward me, remote in her fingers. "You need to see this."

She hits play.

The screen flickers. Then my parents are on the screen, side by side in the office that we just walked back into.

"We should've spoken up sooner," my father says. "And to our daughter—we are sorry. For the silence. For the damage. For letting someone else write her story."

My mother nods. "The things being said about her are false. Reckless. And in Carl's case—criminal. He used our name and our history. That ends now."

"She thought we disowned her once," my dad adds, quietly. "We let our silence make her believe that we are doing that again."

I don't say anything for a second. "They should've said it years ago."

Beckett's voice is low beside me. "They did now. And while the world's watching."

I glance at the banner still crawling beneath the live broadcast.

Hallingsworth Legal Team Declines to Comment. Alexandra Collette remains Unreachable.

Good.

It's over.

Not all of it. Not everything. But the part that mattered most—the part that tried to destroy me.

I breathe. Deep. Solid. The kind that hits the bottom of your lungs and doesn't hurt anymore.

When I look up, the room is still watching—but this time, no one's waiting for me to break.

Talia meets my eyes first. Cal gives me a slow smile, small but proud. Richard—ever the strategist—just tips his head like a man who always knew I'd outplay them.

Stellan watches me like he's seeing a prophecy fulfilled. Like this moment is the one he's been waiting for.

Then there's Beckett.

Right beside me. Like he always has been.

I reach for his hand. This time, I never have to let go.

We walk out together.

No press. No running or hiding.

Just us.

In love, alive, and ready for our lives to begin.

Epilogue
FRANKIE

THERE'S NO PRESS.

No stage lighting. No curated guest list. No designer contract stapled to my bouquet. And no Chapel.

Just a vineyard an hour outside the city, a crooked little aisle made of crushed stone and old rose petals, and the man who's been choosing me—every damn day—since I let him.

Beckett stands at the far end in a charcoal suit that shouldn't make me weak in the knees—but absolutely does. Hands in his pockets. That crooked smile is already forming.

The scent of lavender, stone, and a distant bonfire fill the air, bringing peace in the space. The sun is warm on my shoulders and a soft breeze tugs at the hem of my dress.

My dress is not white. It's ivory, like moonlight, made from soft silk that moves when I breathe. The thin straps and open back make it feel like me, like I can relax, let go, and know that my husband is there to help me along the way. There's a slit up one side, but I didn't wear it for modesty. I wore it to feel free. I could walk this aisle barefoot, alone, unbothered.

But I'm not alone.

My father is next to me.

His arm is firm beneath my hand, but I can feel the tension in him. Not nerves. Not regret. Just—gravity. Like he knows this walk is for both of us.

Stone crunches beneath our shoes. Flower petals scatter. A breeze lifts the edge of my dress like it knows this is the moment everything changes.

Talia stands at the front, holding the rings and trying not to cry. My mother's already losing that battle behind her sunglasses. Cal nods at me like I'm the answer to a question he'd stopped asking. Richard pretends not to be emotional—but I see the way his jaw tightens.

Stellan—of all people—is officiating.

He doesn't open a book. He just glances at us—at me and Beckett—and gives the smallest nod. "Whenever you're ready."

Beckett goes first. He keeps my hand in his. I can't keep my eyes off of me.

"I always kept people at arm's length," he says. "Built walls. Kept everything... contained. That was how I stayed in control."

He looks at me—straight through me.

"But you didn't just break through. You snuck in. Into all my defenses. Every guard I'd ever built. Like you were meant to be there all along."

He shakes his head, just barely.

"I was raised to lead with kindness. To believe softness wasn't weakness, that love—real love—should be loud and everyday and worn proudly. But somewhere along the way, people started twisting that. Taking from it. Taking from me. So I learned to hide that part of myself. To protect it. To bury it so deep I forgot it was there. And then you came in—wild, relentless, impossible to ignore—and without even trying, you pulled it all back out. You didn't just make space for who I am. You reminded me why I ever wanted to be him in the first place. So no, I'm not promising perfection. I'm promising to stay soft. To stay kind. To stay open. With you, always."

Then it's my turn. And I don't look at anyone but him.

"I loved you when I was twenty one," I say, voice wavering slightly, "but I was wrong—I thought love was messy, heat, something that hits fast and dies slowly. I didn't know that real love is something you have to fight for and bleed with and still choose when everything hurts. You stood with me, through every moment, every failure, every time I tried to push you away. So no, I'm not promising easy. I'm promising to always tell you the truth. I'm promising to stay. Because I didn't understand love then—but I do now. And it's still you. It's always been you."

We don't wait for Stellan to say the words.

Beckett kisses me like we've been married for years—like this is just another war we won together.

But this time, I don't feel like I need to wait for the other shoe to drop.

I didn't just give up.

And because of that, I got everything.

Frankie's Bar Playlist

THE SIGNATURE SOUND OF THE DUTCH WALL

1 "FEVER" - PEGGY LEE

    2 "Dreams" - Fleetwood Mac

    3 "Black" - Pearl Jam

    4 "Take Me to Church" - Hozier

    5 "Gimme Shelter" - The Rolling Stones

    6 "Barracuda" - Heart

    7 "Fade Into You" - Mazzy Star

    8 "Go Your Own Way" - Fleetwood Mac

    9 "Seven Nation Army" - The White Stripes

    10 "Summertime" - Ella Fitzgerald & Louis Armstrong

    11 "The Chain" - Fleetwood Mac

    12 "Midnight City" - M83

    13 "Bittersweet Symphony" - The Verve

    14 "I Don't Wanna Live Forever" - ZAYN & Taylor Swift

    15 "Dog Days Are Over" - Florence + The Machine

    16 "Do I Wanna Know?" - Arctic Monkeys

    17 "House of the Rising Sun" - The Animals

    18 "You Know I'm No Good" - Amy Winehouse

    19 "Way Down We Go" - KALEO

20 "Somebody Else" - The 1975

Listen on Spotify: https://open.spotify.com/playlist/398Z9pPp6kvtqRLiRiKu82?si=v6yT3jrTROKLIPDxuFhOoQ

Frankie's Cocktail Recipes

THE HARRINGTON (CLASSIC OLD FASHIONED)
Beckett's drink
Ingredients:
- 2 oz bourbon or rye whiskey
- 1 sugar cube
- 2-3 dashes Angostura bitters
- Orange peel
- Luxardo cherry

Instructions: Place sugar cube in an old fashioned glass and saturate with bitters. Muddle until dissolved. Add whiskey and one large ice cube. Stir for 30 seconds. Express orange peel oils over the drink, then drop it in. Add cherry.

Frankie says: "Beckett orders this every single time. Never changes. Never experiments. It's annoyingly perfect, just like him."

WILDFLOWER & WHISKEY *(Whiskey Sour) Frankie's drink*

Ingredients:

- 2 oz bourbon
- 3/4 oz fresh lemon juice
- 1/2 oz simple syrup
- 1 egg white (optional, for foam)
- Lemon wheel and cherry for garnish

Instructions: Dry shake (without ice) bourbon, lemon juice, simple syrup, and egg white for 10 seconds. Add ice and shake hard for 15 seconds. Strain into a rocks glass over fresh ice. Garnish with lemon wheel and cherry.

Frankie says: "This is me in a glass. Looks sweet, tastes sharp, leaves an impression. The egg white makes it fancy. I'm not fancy, but the drink can be."

THE ARCHITECT *(Sazerac) Stellan's drink*

Ingredients:

- 2 oz rye whiskey
- 1/4 oz simple syrup
- 3 dashes Peychaud's bitters
- Absinthe rinse
- Lemon peel

Instructions: Rinse a chilled old fashioned glass with absinthe, discard excess. In a mixing glass, stir rye, simple syrup, and bitters with ice. Strain into the prepared glass (no ice). Express lemon peel oils over the drink and discard peel.

Frankie says: "I knew Stellan needed something with

history. Something most people don't order because they're too intimidated. He wasn't. He never is."

GOLDEN HOUR *(French 75) Talia's drink*

Ingredients:

- 1 oz gin
- 1/2 oz fresh lemon juice
- 1/2 oz simple syrup
- 3 oz champagne
- Lemon twist

Instructions: Shake gin, lemon juice, and simple syrup with ice. Strain into a champagne flute. Top with champagne. Garnish with lemon twist.

Frankie says: "Light, sophisticated, celebratory. Talia drinks this and somehow makes everyone else feel more elegant too. It's a gift."

THE NIGHT SHIFT *(Spicy Margarita) Roxy's drink*

Ingredients:

- 2 oz silver tequila
- 1 oz fresh lime juice
- 3/4 oz Cointreau
- 2-3 slices jalapeño
- Tajín or salt rim
- Lime wheel

Instructions: Muddle jalapeño slices in a shaker. Add tequila, lime juice, and Cointreau with ice. Shake hard. Rim glass with Tajín or salt. Strain into prepared rocks glass over fresh ice. Garnish with lime wheel.

Frankie says: "Roxy doesn't do boring. This has kick, color, and attitude. Just like her. She usually orders two."

THE MANAGER *(Espresso Martini) Lena's drink*

Ingredients:

- 2 oz vodka
- 1 oz Kahlúa
- 1 oz fresh espresso (cooled)
- 1/2 oz simple syrup
- 3 coffee beans for garnish

Instructions: Shake all ingredients vigorously with ice until frothy and cold. Strain into a chilled martini glass. Garnish with three coffee beans.

Frankie says: "Lena runs this place like a machine. Smooth, strong, never fails. This is her fuel. I make it exactly the same way every time. She notices if I don't."

THE LEGACY *(Manhattan) Richard's drink*

Ingredients:

- 2 oz rye whiskey
- 1 oz sweet vermouth

- 2 dashes Angostura bitters
- Luxardo cherry

Instructions: Stir whiskey, vermouth, and bitters with ice until well chilled. Strain into a coupe or martini glass. Garnish with cherry.

Frankie says: "Richard taught Beckett how to drink like a gentleman. This is what he orders when he wants to remind everyone he built an empire from nothing. It works."

Frankie's Mocktail Recipes

THE VEGAS SPECIAL *(VIRGIN PIÑA COLADA)*
Ingredients:
- 2 oz coconut cream
- 3 oz pineapple juice
- 1/2 oz fresh lime juice
- Pineapple wedge and cherry for garnish

Instructions: Blend coconut cream, pineapple juice, and lime juice with ice until smooth. Pour into a hurricane glass. Garnish with pineapple wedge and cherry.

Frankie says: "This is what we should've been drinking in Vegas. Sweet, tropical, ridiculous. Would've saved us a lot of trouble. Or at least I would've remembered the wedding."

THE CELEBRATION *(Virgin Mojito)*
Ingredients:
- 8-10 fresh mint leaves

- 1 oz fresh lime juice
- 1 oz simple syrup
- Club soda
- Lime wheel and mint sprig for garnish

Instructions: Muddle mint leaves gently in a highball glass. Add lime juice and simple syrup. Fill glass with ice. Top with club soda and stir gently. Garnish with lime wheel and mint sprig.

Frankie says: "Fresh, bright, makes you feel fancy without the hangover. Perfect for when you're celebrating but need to drive home. Talia's go to these days."

LAST CALL *(Shirley Temple)*

Ingredients:

- 4 oz ginger ale or lemon-lime soda
- 1/2 oz grenadine
- Maraschino cherry and orange slice for garnish

Instructions: Fill glass with ice. Add ginger ale or soda. Pour grenadine down the side of the glass. Stir gently. Garnish with cherry and orange slice.

Frankie says: "Don't let the name fool you. This is a classic for a reason. Sweet, bubbly, nostalgic. I make these for regulars who want something easy at the end of the night."

THE APOLOGY *(Roy Rogers)*

Ingredients:
- 4 oz cola
- 1/2 oz grenadine
- Maraschino cherry for garnish

Instructions: Fill glass with ice. Add cola. Pour grenadine down the side of the glass. Stir gently. Garnish with cherry.

Frankie says: "The Shirley Temple's cowboy cousin. Simple, sweet, gets the job done. This is what I make when someone screws up and needs something to hold while they apologize. Usually works."

CLASSIC FRENCH OMELET

This is what I made for Frankie the morning we decided to stop fighting and start building something real. My mother taught me this when I was twelve. She said a man who can make a proper omelet will never go hungry—and never be alone.

Serves: 1

Ingredients:

- 3 large eggs
- 1 tablespoon butter
- Salt and white pepper to taste
- Fresh herbs (chives, tarragon, or parsley), optional
- Gruyère or your preferred cheese, optional

Instructions:

1 Crack eggs into a bowl. Whisk vigorously for 30 seconds until completely uniform—no streaks of white or yolk should remain.

2 Heat an 8-inch nonstick pan over medium heat. Add butter and swirl to coat the entire surface.

3 Once butter foams but hasn't browned, pour in the eggs. Let them sit undisturbed for 5 seconds.

4 Using a silicone spatula, gently push the edges toward the center while tilting the pan to let uncooked egg flow to the edges. Repeat until the eggs are mostly set but still slightly wet on top.

5 If using cheese or herbs, add them now to one half of the omelet.

6 Remove from heat. Fold the omelet in half (or in thirds, French style). Slide onto a warm plate.

7 Season with salt and white pepper.

Note: The key is low, steady heat and constant movement. Patience matters here. Don't rush it.

PAN SEARED SALMON WITH LEMON BUTTER

This is my date night plan for Frankie. Something elegant but not pretentious. Something that shows effort without looking like I'm trying too hard. She claims she doesn't need to be impressed. I cook this anyway.

Serves: 2

Ingredients:

- 2 salmon fillets (6 oz each), skin-on, room temperature
- 2 tablespoons olive oil
- Salt and pepper
- 3 tablespoons butter
- 2 cloves garlic, minced
- Juice of 1 lemon
- Fresh parsley, chopped
- Lemon wedges for serving

Instructions:

1 Pat salmon completely dry with paper towels. Season both sides generously with salt and pepper.

2 Heat olive oil in a large skillet over medium-high heat until it shimmers.

3 Place salmon in the pan skin-side down. Press gently with a spatula for 10 seconds to ensure even contact.

4 Cook without moving for 4-5 minutes until the skin is crispy and the salmon is cooked halfway up the sides.

5 Flip carefully and cook for another 2-3 minutes for medium doneness.

6 Remove salmon to a plate and tent with foil.

7 In the same pan, reduce heat to medium. Add butter and garlic. Cook until fragrant, about 30 seconds.

8 Add lemon juice and swirl to combine. Remove from heat.

9 Pour sauce over salmon. Garnish with parsley and lemon wedges.

Note: Don't overcook the salmon. It should still be slightly translucent in the center when you remove it from heat. It will continue cooking as it rests. Frankie prefers hers medium. I've learned not to argue.

SUNDAY ROAST BEEF

My father and I make this together every few months. It's tradition. He carves, I make the Yorkshire pudding, and we pretend we're not both avoiding talking about anything emotional. It works for us.

Serves: 6-8

Ingredients:

- 1 boneless ribeye roast (4-5 lbs)
- 4 tablespoons softened butter
- 4 cloves garlic, minced
- 2 tablespoons fresh rosemary, chopped
- 2 tablespoons fresh thyme, chopped
- Salt and pepper
- 2 cups beef stock

Instructions:

1 Remove roast from refrigerator 2 hours before cooking. Pat dry.

2 Preheat oven to 450°F.

3 Mix butter, garlic, rosemary, and thyme. Rub all over the roast.

4 Season heavily with salt and pepper.

5 Place roast on a rack in a roasting pan. Pour beef stock into the bottom of the pan.

6 Roast at 450°F for 15 minutes to develop a crust.

7 Reduce heat to 325°F. Continue roasting for 1-1.5 hours, or until internal temperature reaches 125°F for medium-rare (135°F for medium).

8 Remove from oven and tent with foil. Rest for 20 minutes before carving.

9 Slice thinly against the grain.

Note: My father insists on medium-rare. I agree. Use a meat thermometer—guessing leads to disappointment. The drippings make excellent gravy. Don't waste them.

MY MOTHER'S LEMON CAKE

She made this for every birthday. Mine, my father's, anyone she loved. It's simple, but it tastes like coming home. I made it for my dad's birthday last year. He cried. I haven't told anyone that part.

Serves: 8-10

Ingredients:

For the cake:

- 1½ cups all-purpose flour
- 1½ teaspoons baking powder
- ½ teaspoon salt
- 1 cup unsalted butter, softened
- 1 cup granulated sugar
- 4 large eggs
- 2 teaspoons vanilla extract
- Zest of 2 lemons
- ⅓ cup fresh lemon juice
- ½ cup whole milk

For the glaze:

- 1 cup powdered sugar
- 3 tablespoons fresh lemon juice
- Zest of 1 lemon

Instructions:

1 Preheat oven to 350°F. Grease and flour a 9-inch round cake pan.

2 Whisk together flour, baking powder, and salt. Set aside.

3 Cream butter and sugar until light and fluffy, about 3 minutes.

4 Add eggs one at a time, beating well after each addition.

5 Mix in vanilla, lemon zest, and lemon juice.

6 Alternate adding flour mixture and milk, beginning and ending with flour. Mix until just combined.

7 Pour batter into prepared pan. Smooth the top.

8 Bake for 35-40 minutes, or until a toothpick inserted in the center comes out clean.

9 Cool in pan for 10 minutes, then turn out onto a wire rack.

10 For the glaze: whisk powdered sugar, lemon juice, and zest until smooth. Drizzle over warm cake.

Note: The cake is best served slightly warm. My mother would slice it while it was still cooling and hand me a piece with a glass of cold milk. I do the same when I make it now.

WEEKNIGHT PASTA

This is what I make when we're both exhausted and neither of us wants to think. It takes fifteen minutes and requires almost no effort. Frankie says it's cheating. I say it's efficiency.

Serves: 2

Ingredients:
- ½ lb spaghetti
- 3 tablespoons olive oil
- 4 cloves garlic, thinly sliced
- ½ teaspoon red pepper flakes
- ½ cup pasta water (reserved)
- ¼ cup fresh parsley, chopped
- ½ cup grated Parmesan
- Salt and pepper
- Lemon wedges (optional)

Instructions:

1 Cook pasta in salted boiling water until al dente. Reserve ½ cup pasta water before draining.

2 While pasta cooks, heat olive oil in a large skillet over medium heat.

3 Add garlic and red pepper flakes. Cook until garlic is golden and fragrant, about 2 minutes. Do not burn.

4 Add drained pasta to the skillet. Toss to coat in the garlic oil.

5 Add pasta water a little at a time, tossing constantly, until a light sauce forms.

6 Remove from heat. Add parsley and Parmesan. Toss until combined.

7 Season with salt and pepper. Serve with lemon wedges if desired.

Note: This is deceptively simple, which means every ingredient matters. Use good olive oil. Use fresh garlic. Don't skip the pasta water—it's what makes the sauce. Frankie adds extra red pepper flakes.

Bonus Epilogue

WANT MORE FRANKIE & BECKETT?

Download an exclusive **epilogue from Beckett's POV.**

Get the bonus scene at: https://BookHip.com/ XCSQVPP

Also By

The Devil's Bargain

Wicked Union– A prequel novella (Liora and Evander's story)

The Devil's Canvas

Gilded Lies

The Shadow Brides

Veil of Fire

Wildflowers & Whiskey (1.5)

The Huntington Brothers Series

Destined for Love

Tangled Hearts

Promises to Keep

Standalone Novels

The Keeper's Secret

Love on the Edge

Anthologies

Head in the Clouds: A Romantic Comedy Anthology

Desperate: A Deadly Thriller Anthology

Did you love Wildflowers & Whiskey? If you enjoyed the story, I would be so grateful if you took a moment to leave a quick review. Thank you for reading, for your support, and for spending time with these characters. I can't wait for you to see what happens next!

About the Author

SARA MCCLAFLIN WRITES ROMANCE WITH FEELINGS, flaws, and just the right amount of emotional damage. Her stories are character-driven, morally gray, and often ask one very important question: what if love was a little dangerous—and we liked it that way? After years of reading and reviewing books with too much angst, she finally started writing her own.

She lives on the West Coast with her husband, their chaotic dog, and more book boyfriends than she's willing to admit. Her TBR pile is a cry for help, her playlists are 80% heartbreak, and she's always chasing the next character who'll ruin her in the best way.

Newsletter Sign Up:https://subscribepage.io/saras-newsletter